MW00470723

A Broken People's Playlist

A Broken People's Playlist

STORIES (FROM SONGS)

Chimeka Garricks

HARPERVIA

An Imprint of HarperCollins*Publishers*

This is a work of fiction. Names, characters, places, and incidents are products of the author's imagination or are used fictitiously and are not to be construed as real. Any resemblance to actual events, locales, organizations, or persons, living or dead, is entirely coincidental.

A BROKEN PEOPLE'S PLAYLIST. Copyright © 2020 by Chimeka Garricks. All rights reserved. Printed in the United States of America. No part of this book may be used or reproduced in any manner whatsoever without written permission except in the case of brief quotations embodied in critical articles and reviews. For information, address HarperCollins Publishers, 195 Broadway, New York, NY 10007.

HarperCollins books may be purchased for educational, business, or sales promotional use. For information, please email the Special Markets Department at SPsales@harpercollins.com.

Originally published as *A Broken People's Playlist* in Nigeria in 2020 by Masobe Books.

FIRST HARPERONE HARDCOVER PUBLISHED IN 2023

Designed by Terry McGrath

Library of Congress Cataloging-in-Publication Data has been applied for.

ISBN 978-0-06-326818-0

23 24 25 26 27 LBC 5 4 3 2 1

HB 01.12.2023 1253

For the unforgettables: Chris, Morgan, Wabiye, U, and Dame

and

the irreplaceables: Biyai, Ebinabo, Kala-Wabiye, and Uwhetu

Track List

"Lost Stars"*

They will ask me when I first knew I was in love with you. I will sigh and say I don't know.

It happened in fragments, piece by piece, separate moments over the years. Moments—that's how I remember it.

They will be surprised when I say you are the only man I have loved.

I hear that familiar whistle from my teens, and know it is you. I smile, and my legs pull me, past my parents' suspicious looks, out to the balcony. You are downstairs on the street, looking up at me with your smile, still cheeky.

I haven't seen you in almost two years since the last time I was in Port Harcourt. I make a show of folding my arms. "Hey!" I say. "You can't still be whistling to call me. Don't you have a phone?"

"Next time I whistle, you better come out fast."

---

* Written under the influence of "Lost Stars" by Adam Levine

"Wait o! Because you're now riding okada, you think you can talk to me anyhow?"

"Bush woman. This is not an okada." You pat the black and silver motorcycle you are sitting astride. "This is a Triumph Thunderb—"

"Ehn, your mates who drive cars—do they have two heads?"

"I have a car. Or rather, a van, but I use it to deliver eggs from my farm. It's either that or this. Choose one."

"I'm not choosing any."

"Let's go. Lunch. There's this buka on Station Road. I promise, you'll sell your soul for their Fisherman's Soup."

"You want to take me to a buka on an okada? You can't be serious."

"Your mates who eat in bukas and ride okadas—do they have two heads?" You look at your wrist, which doesn't have a watch. "You're wasting time."

"Come up and greet my parents while I think about it."

You smile. "Still using me, abi?" But you get off the motorcycle.

"I'll use you more in the next few days. Besides, you enjoy it."

"Beg me first."

"You'll die of old age if you're waiting for me to beg."

You sigh and get back on the motorcycle.

We stare at each other till I say, "Okay. You win. Abeg now."

"How long are you in town for?"

"Till a week from today. Monday, after the wedding." Nua, my immediate younger sister, is getting married on Saturday. "You're coming, right?"

"Of course."

I add, "And for the Thanksgiving on Sunday too?"

You nod.

"Thanks."

We'd gone by taxi. The buka had almost emptied out from the lunchtime crowd by the time we arrived. It was clean though, meaning we didn't have to swat flies from sharing our food. The Fisherman's Soup was good, but I'd had better. I told you so. After eating, we sit back on the wooden benches while waiting for you to finish your Gulder. I take sips from your glass. The beer is almost flat, and I don't enjoy it. But I keep sipping. "My mother was cold to you today."

You chuckle. "She saw me with a girl the other day on my bike. She's been carrying face for me since then." You tilt the glass as you pour the last of the beer from the bottle. "I don't blame her sha. She thinks we've been dating for two years, I've not shown any intention to marry you, and I'm carrying girls all over town."

After Nua's wedding, I'd be the only one among the four sisters in my family who wasn't married. And at thirty-five, I am the oldest. It was a prayer point for my mother and the starting point for our many battles. I sip more beer. "I'm sorry. That's how she is."

"After this wedding, perhaps you should stop acting like we're dating."

I sigh. "I only do it when I'm in Port Harcourt." I add, "I'm sorry this is cramping your style with your girlfriend."

You smile. "You're not sorry. And she's not my girlfriend."

"Who's she?"

You shrug. "We meet each other's needs. You know how these things are. She's not important. Wait! You're jealous?"

"No!" I hiss. "You wish."

Your smile says you don't believe me.

I point at you. "It's you who's jealous."

"Me? Jealous? Of who? Femi?"

"Yes. You've always been jealous of Femi."

"His money? Yes. Him? No." You chuckle. "How're you and Femi sef?"

I pause before I answer. "We're fine."

"How many years have you guys . . ."

Your words trail off, but I know what you're asking.

"We've been together for over four years, thank you very much." I hear the irritation in my voice.

You raise your glass to your lips, but before you drink, you cut me with, "Still believe that he's about to leave his wife?"

You drink. I don't answer. You leave some beer in the glass and signal-ask if I want it. I shake my head.

"I'm sorry," you say.

"You're not sorry."

You smile. "You're right. I'm not."

We never quite happened, but everyone assumed we did. Even from when we were teens.

Although we both grew up in D-line and saw each other around the neighbourhood, we first met in '97. You were nineteen, in uni; I was seventeen, about to get in. Your father's bakery was down the road from our house, though your family lived on the next street. You worked at the bakery, evenings and holidays, sometimes over the counter where you handed out soft, warm loaves and shy smiles. You stopped smiling when your father died. He was a well-liked man, and the neighbourhood pulled together for your mum. That was when my mother and your mum became close. And when she brought me along for one of her many visits, you and I first talked. It was nothing, just awkward commiserations and silence. Then, on a balmy day in July, I accompanied my mother to your father's funeral in Omoku, and I remember being struck by how you, the last child, stayed deadpan while your mum and siblings wailed and thrashed as they lowered the casket. Weeks later, my mother sent me to drop off a big cooler of jollof rice at your house. I walked into what looked like a meeting in the living room involving your mum, elder brothers, and some older men. As you helped me take the cooler to the kitchen, you quickly wiped away a tear, but I'd seen it. You were as surprised as I was when I asked you to walk me back home. Till today, I don't know what pushed those words out of my mouth. All I knew was I could sense you needed to be somewhere else at that moment.

Rather than go to my house, we ended up strolling through more than half of D-line, crisscrossing the railway line twice at the Fruit Garden Market and at the bole and fish stalls at Agudama Street, and even heading up as far as the close on Udom Street and U-turning in front of Hotel Chez Therese. Somewhere on that walk, you told me how your uncles were demanding ownership of the bakery from your mum. I talked of my parents' unhappy marriage, how I eavesdrop on my mother when she goes to cry in the bathroom, and how I didn't get along with any of them. You didn't talk about your father. I didn't talk about Victor, my boyfriend at the time.

But Victor's friends had seen us walking. Later, he was with two of them when he asked me about it. I said it was nothing. He said I was lying. He said I was "perambulating" around D-line with you and embarrassing him. I said he was overreacting. I even apologised. Then he slapped me.

I was used to my father beating my mother. He did it almost with a nonchalance that came from regular practice and confidence in her perpetual surrender. But I am not my mother. I slapped Victor so hard, my wrist almost snapped, and the pain jolted up my arm. By the time his friends succeeded in pulling him off me, my face was bloodied, my top torn, and my ears rung with, "Ashawo! Ashawo!" which was what he'd been screaming at me.

The beating didn't hurt as much as the stories I heard afterwards. I heard I slept with Victor, then with three of his friends, then with you, then with every man who winked at me. Some of the stories had specific details—places, dates, and one even had the colour of my panties. I don't know how, but somehow, the stories found my parents' ears one day. That evening, my father's tirade lashed me till I red-misted and answered back. That was the first time he told me to leave his house.

You didn't seem surprised when I turned up at your room at the BQ behind your parents' house that night. You didn't ask why I was there, and I wasn't in the mood to talk. I flicked through your photo album, books, and music collection. You played your homemade CDs—Smokie, U2, Bon Jovi, Oasis—tuning me to rock for the first time. You got me dinner—fluffy bread, Blue Band margarine, and thick, sweetened Milo. I smiled because you dipped your bread in the cocoa before eating. You convinced me to try it when you joked that it was more than comfort food—it was also one of the secrets to happiness. You watched me do it, and the expression on my face confirmed you were right. You laughed. It was the first time I heard that infectious rumble. It prised a chuckle from me, and the simple magic of everything flipped my mood. I told you everything. You didn't say anything for a long time. We lay on your mattress on the floor and stared unabashedly at each other, but it was soothing, intimate. Inevitably, still in silence, we cosied up till I rested my head on your chest, feeling your heart pound as you stroked my hair. Looking back, I wish I had bottled the peace of that moment and carried it through my life.

We were still in each other's arms when your mum, without knocking, pushed open the door. My mother was behind her. I trudged home in silence beside my mother. She didn't speak to me till the next morning when she banned me from talking to you. I managed to obey for only one month. I wish I rebelled sooner.

Years later, we would talk about that night and play out what might have been. We agreed that we would have made love. You tell me that you'd wanted to, but you were reluctant to make a move when I was vulnerable. I tell you that it would have been my first time. I don't tell you that I'd hoped you'd been my first, and I still wish you were. My first was Victor, who came to apologise the next day and every day for almost two weeks. I blanked him until the day someone told me about Osa, your then girlfriend. I didn't tell you that I cried, snuck to Victor's house, mechanically took off my clothes, and lay zombied on his bed. I tell you I wish you'd told me about Osa that night. You tell me you would have mentioned her, but our mothers came in. You also tell me you'd organised for some guys to beat up Victor, but you called it off when you realised we were dating again. I shrug and don't tell you that I wish you hadn't called it off.

But I tell you that anytime I get blue, I eat bread dipped in Milo, and it makes everything better.

They will ask me how often I told you I love you. And I will sigh and say I don't recall ever saying it. But you knew.

You knew those times when you'd look up and catch me watching you, and I'd refuse to look away. You knew in your darkest days—when you missed your father, when your uncles took over the bakery and ran it down, when your family's money ran out, when you didn't have a job, when the depression smothered you, and you wished for death to end it all—you came to me to hold you till some light pierced through. You knew on those nights when I called you, after Femi had gone home to his wife, after I'd dried my tears, and you made me laugh, talked me to sleep, and lied that everything would be okay.

You were cutting my hair when you proposed.

It was the Thursday before Nua's church wedding. On Monday, after the buka visit, you finally convinced me to get on your motorcycle, and we rode—you weaving through traffic, me shrieking parts of the way—to your farm in Igwuruta. There I watched, fascinated by the incongruous sights of you, guy-man, walking through the poultry house, feeding fish in the tanks, and calling a king boar "Oga" at the outdoor pigpen. Between brief meetings with your workers, you talked about how after years of unsuccessfully looking for work, you became an accidental farmer, starting small with a tiny poultry behind your mum's house. You beamed as you talked about how well the farm was doing, how surprised you were that you were enjoying running it, and how you seemed to have found your place in the world. I said you looked like you were finally at peace with yourself. Your smile was shy, and for a second, I caught a glimpse of the boy from the bakery. And my heart was suddenly full because I'd never loved you as much as I did at that moment.

The ride back to the city that night wasn't as hairy, and when you dropped me off at my parents' house, just like old times, you walked me to the door and kissed me easily. I warned you not to kiss me that casually as if the last time we kissed was ten minutes before and not three years, five months, and two days ago. You asked if I'd really been counting. I told you to stop being silly. You laughed, and we kissed properly till I accidentally leaned on the doorbell. The next day, I went with my family to Bori for Nua's traditional wedding, which was scheduled for Wednesday. You came with your mum to Bori for the ceremony and rolled your eyes as she bear-hugged me and made you take pictures as we pouted and posed. As a pretend boyfriend, you were perfect—spending as much time with me as possible and even briefly sitting under a canopy with my brothers-in-law, the husbands of my two youngest sisters, where you smirked and made faces at me.

When I returned on Thursday, I went to your flat at Stadium Road. Famished, we didn't make it to your bedroom. We tore at each other's clothes but gave up midway and merged half-dressed on your living-room wall. As your face headed down between my legs, as always, we paused for a moment and chuckled because we remembered—the first time you ate me, my first time ever, I farted uncontrollably through a long orgasm, and you rolled off and laughed till I joined in. Thursday was kisses, bites, sweat, thrusts, and screams—a frenzied mauling because there was no tomorrow. Liquid electric, it coursed through every cell, jolting my body alive, but felt good for my spirit like a homecoming.

Eventually, we collapsed to the floor beside your door. After, we stumbled to your room where we drank wine, cuddled, and ribbed each other. Then we did it again, slower, bodies rhyming gently because of scarred souls. Then we napped (different sides of the bed because I disliked being cuddled when I slept), woke, and talked. It was when you touched my head that I realised my wig had fallen off.

I'd developed alopecia when I turned nineteen. By twenty, I'd lost almost all my hair apart from ugly patches, which were so irregular and sparse, I couldn't even wear weaves. You went with me to buy wigs, helped me choose, and deliberately cracked the unfunniest jokes when I cried so I'd get annoyed enough to hit you and stop crying. Then, you started cutting my hair regularly, balding my head. And when I got confident enough, you accompanied me to barbershops. At the time, you were still dating Osa, I'd long moved on from Victor, and technically, we hadn't yet crossed the line, but our "just friends" shtick didn't fool anyone.

You ran your hand through my tufts.

I said, "So . . . you're waiting for me to ask you to cut my hair, abi?"

"I've stopped cutting hair for free. Especially for ungrateful women."

"Ah, sorry o. Cut it first. I'll prostrate in gratitude later."

You shook your head and sighed like you always did when you had no comeback. And that was how I ended up sitting in your bathroom, naked except for the barber's cape over me, watching in the big mirror while you cut my hair with your electric clippers. We stared at each other in the mirror.

"Sira."

"Yes?"

"I'm tired."

"Ahn-ahn, you just started cutting."

"No. I'm tired of being your friend and occasional fuck-buddy."

"Correction. Best friend and my One Who Got Away."

"For the record, I never went away."

"You know what I mean. Our timings are always wrong. I'll be available. You'll be dating someone. Vice versa. I keep telling you—it's like we aren't fated to be."

"Nonsense. We were together once."

"Yes, but that was for just the three weeks before I moved to Lagos."

"Best three weeks of my life."

"Me too."

You sighed. "I wish you didn't move."

"Why didn't you ask me not to?"

"C'mon now. Since I knew you, you always wanted to leave home. Remember those times you talked about running away, and I yabbed you because running away only works in oyibo movies? And you finished school, finished NYSC, got this dream job. I didn't yet have a job, we knew we weren't built for long-distance crap. . . ." Your shoulders slumped.

"Another correction—I wanted to leave home, leave this city, only because all that shit with Victor messed up my reputation. Aaand . . . ," I mimicked your voice and did air quotes, "for the record, you didn't ask." I shrugged.

You stooped and flicked the clipper off as the realisation hit you. "You would have stayed if I asked?"

I smiled. "For someone who knows me as well as you do, you ask silly questions sometimes." I sighed. "So, you're tired of being my friend. What are you really trying to say—that we should stop talking? Because, let me warn you, it won't work."

"Now you're being the silly one." You fluffed hair off my head with a duster, leaned forward from behind me, and kissed my scalp. You held my eyes in the mirror.

"I want more. I want everything. Marry me, Sira."

They will ask me why I said no. And I will sigh and say exactly what I told you—because I wasn't a child anymore, and because I knew love alone was never enough in this life.

You said you didn't understand. I explained that we'd both moved on. I was in Lagos about to be announced as a partner in the law firm where I'd worked for years; you were in Port Harcourt running a growing farm business that required your presence. I told you I didn't want to give up my life and move back to Port Harcourt, and I would eventually resent you if I did. I told you I wouldn't forgive myself if you gave up your life and all you'd worked hard for, for me. You said we would work out something. I told you not to be naïve.

Then you said I sounded materialistic.

There was an unspoken undercurrent to that statement—years ago, you'd "joked" that I was with Femi because he was rich, and I felt this statement was a continuation of that jibe.

So, I told you to fuck off. And I left your flat. And I refused to see you on Friday. And I was cold to you all through Nua's wedding on Saturday as well as during the Thanksgiving on Sunday. And I refused to answer your calls or reply to your messages.

And before I left on Monday morning, I told my mother the truth—about us, about Femi, about Victor, about my relationship with her. Her face was inscrutable when I finished talking and remained so when she held me, suddenly, woodenly, because it had been years since we'd hugged, and we'd forgotten how. Then, voice strong and lifted, she said a long, lyrical, heartfelt prayer for me in Khana, not English—because Nigerian mothers don't apologise in conventional ways.

"Hey. Good morning."

"Hey, stranger."

"Behave. It's just ten days."

"Feels like ten years."

"So, I need to talk to you. Right now."

"You think you can walk out of my life and walk in anytime you like, abi?"

"I know I can."

You chuckled. "Okay."

"They just made me partner. Signed the partnership agreement ten minutes ago. Formal announcement and notices to clients tomorrow. Party on Saturday."

"Yay! Congratulations."

I shrugged. "Thanks."

"Are you okay?"

"I'm just . . . I don't know what to feel. I slaved for this for years. I've finally gotten it, and honestly, it feels a bit empty. Like, is this all? Is this life? Right now, I'm making this call from the toilet in my office because I can't stand people congratulating me. Is this normal?"

"Are you sure it's not PMS that is doing you?"

I guffawed. "No. I just finished my period."

"Hunger, nko?"

"I just had breakfast."

"Okay o." You sighed. "Try not to worry too much. These things happen. You'll probably feel better later."

"Are you sure?"

"No. I'm just saying this shit because it sounds nice."

"Thanks for nothing." But I was smiling into my phone.

"You're welcome." Pause. "I'm sorry, Sira."

"I know. I'm sorry too. I overreacted."

"You think?"

"Don't push it."

"So, I've got news. I found a guy."

"What guy?"

"I found a guy who's going to manage my farm and the workers when I'm away. Trustworthy guy. All his references check out. People say only good things about him."

"Why do you want someone managing your farm?"

"So I can move to Lagos. I'll call him every day, double-check everything he does with my customers, and go to Port Harcourt twice or thrice a month to see how things are. I also plan to buy land in Lagos for another farm." There was silence for a while. "Sira, I was serious when I said we can make this work. I'm willing to do what it takes."

I felt the bird's wings beating furiously where my heart used to be.

"Sira?"

"Yes."

"Say something."

I exhaled. "Like I said, my firm's throwing a party on Saturday for me here in Lagos. Are you coming?"

"Only if you ask nicely."

"I need you. Please."

"That's shameless emotional blackmail. But it works. I'll be there."

"Thanks. You can stay at my place. You don't have to get a hotel."

"Sure."

"And, in case you were wondering, I broke up with Femi last week."

It was a long time before you spoke. "Why? How?"

"It was the right time." I sighed. "I'll give you the details when we see."

"Okay."

"Cool. I've got to go now."

"Okay. Talk soon."

"Wait . . ."

Till today, I don't know what made me tell you then because I'd planned to wait till I saw you. But looking back, I'm glad I did.

"Kaodini?"

"Yes?"

"Yes."

"Yes what?"

"Yes, I'll marry you, Kaodini. You're welcome."

You don't come to Lagos. The party was cancelled.

Later that day, as you rode from your farm, a commuter bus that was parked by the kerb suddenly swung into the road without the driver indicating. It slapped your motorcycle off its course, and it careened into the concrete median strip that divided the road. But the force flung you over to the other lane where your body was quickly mangled by oncoming traffic. Your helmet protected your head, and this kept you conscious long enough to call me as they sped you to the hospital. 4:17 p.m.

I saw the call, but I didn't answer it because I was in a meeting.

I called you after, but you didn't answer. 5:42 p.m.

I get a call from your phone. 6:33 p.m.

I answer it. "Hey, baby."

"Sira, it's me o." It was your mum. As soon as I heard her voice, the crack in it, I knew.

"Hello, Ma. Where's Kaodini?"

"My daughter, I hope you're sitting down."

"Yyyes, Ma."

"Hmm, Sira. My baby, our baby. He is dead."

Two years later, they don't ask me why I resigned from my job or why I walk around without my wigs. They don't ask why I moved back to Port Harcourt to your apartment, piled your clothes on the bed, and lay in them for days. They don't talk about the time I fought my mother and sisters and your mum, when they came to drag me off the bed, give me a bath, and wash your clothes and your scent off them. They don't talk about my display at your funeral, where I flung myself at your casket. They don't ask me why I became an insomniac or why for weeks, the only thing I ate was bread dipped in Milo. They don't talk about why I'm in therapy.

Gradually, they've learned that I like it when they talk about you. So, they do. They ask questions about everything—about how we met, how I first knew I was in love with you, how often I told you, how you proposed.

Today, they even asked me why I love you. And I sighed and said because even though we weren't meant to be, you were always home to me.

"Music"*

As I got home and saw my father dancing, I knew there was trouble.

He danced all the time. Usually, it was slow, gentle head sways and occasional shoulder burps—but always without rhythm. It didn't matter if the song was fast or slow or if the bass bombed eardrums. He'd trance-dance, eyes closed, like he, only he, could hear a deeper sound, something hidden under the melodies, chords, and percussions.

That evening was different. He still lacked rhythm, but there was some strutting, arm waving, and yansh wagging. And he sang. A song was playing. He sang over it with a jarring baritone. I chased the music for a moment and then caught it. Victor Uwaifo. From the cassette deck. Not the record player. It meant one thing—it was the Highlife tape I had made for him.

He sang the famous lyric of never running away if you see a mami water.

And I knew. The song was his gift to my mother—a dagger thrust.

---

* Written under the influence of "Music" by Erick Sermon & Marvin Gaye

She winced. I remember thinking that at least it was a change from her usual glare. My mother was so proud of her temper that she wore frowns like medals of honour. She stood, arms folded, by the bookshelf in the living room. Majikpo, my elder brother and mini frowner, was next to her, fully clenched in jaw, fists, and probably arsehole too. He looked ready, eager even, to fight our father if she told him to. Chi Girl, baby sister, sat on the three-seater couch by herself. Her head was a pendulum, watching everybody, trying to stay neutral. I could see she was about to cry. I slunk into the house, went to her, tugged one of her plaits, sat down, and put an arm around her. Her two-armed return hug hurt my ribs.

I kept my sigh quiet. "Why are they fighting again?"

She murmured, "Because of Daddy and Ms. Ukor." Then she leaned even closer. Half-sitting, half-kneeling, she cupped my ear and whispered, "Mummy was like, Ms. Ukor is a witch. And Daddy was like, no, she's not a witch. Then Daddy said Mummy's jealous because Ms. Ukor is fine like mami water. And then he started playing this song. And rewinding it and playing it again."

I smiled.

Afterwards, my mother would harangue me for that smile. And I would lie and say that I'd grinned because my father began playing air guitar at that same moment.

"Guitar Boy!"

But because mothers are usually built to know when their sons are trying to play wayo, she didn't believe me. And because my mother was legally allowed to blame me for anything she felt like, somehow, the unspoken verdict was that my smile was the last straw, leading to what happened next.

She strode to the cassette player. She killed the music with a vicious two-fingered stab of the Eject button, bypassing Stop. The death throes, a dull whirring, were also cut short as she yanked out the cassette. She snarled as she disembowelled it—pulling, spilling, and cutting spool—with her hands and once, with her teeth. Not satisfied, she threw the dead cassette on the ground, raised her bathroom-slippered sole, and stomped it. Twice.

It had taken me a long time to make that mixtape. I had dubbed it from several Highlife vinyl records, many of which I'd borrowed from reluctant owners and music studios. Till today, I've been unable to remake that playlist, and I still have it in my head. The A Side, which I dubbed "the naughty side," started with "Guitar Boy (Mami Water)," which was why my father rewound it easily, followed by Cardinal Rex Jim Lawson's "Sawale" and Bobby Benson's "Taxi Driver." The B Side, "the philosophical side," opened with Chief Osita Osadebe's "Osondi Owendi," Nico Mbarga's "Sweet Mother," and William Onyeabor's "When the Going Is Smooth and Good." Till today, I mourn that playlist.

My father had been playing his air guitar when the music stopped. My mother had also succeeded in ending his singing. He stood frozen, fingers hung mid-strum in the air, looking both menacing and ridiculous. They glared at each other for a long, terrible moment, their eyes eloquently speaking of the mutual hatred. We, the three children, stiffened, waiting for the fight to the death, which was sure to happen. I remember that I'd planned to take Chi Girl to her room and cover her ears with my Walkman, as always.

We waited.

Instead of fighting my mother as he'd normally do, my father did something unexpected that day—something that hurt her a lot more than any of his blows ever would.

He smiled. It was black, bitter, like bile. Then he sang, louder this time, about never running away if he, Amezhi Thomas, sees a mami water.

My father won that day's battle.

Seyi crossfaded from "Play That Funky Music" to "O.P.P." He was rewarded with approving squeals from the teenagers on the dance floor. It was packed, with little space to squirm but not enough to dance. Seyi smiled, hung the earphones on his neck, and shouted in my ear. "Aburo, you know I can't let you play? Big S says so—you know na."

It was 1991. I was seventeen, a year out of secondary school because I hadn't scored high enough in my first JAMB exam to get admission into a university. From the time I was fifteen in SS2, I'd been working part-time, mainly weekends, at the Music Factory Studios owned by Soki, or Big S as everyone, including his mother, called him. I had started small—running errands to buy food, smokes, and drinks for the DJs, cleaning the place, and hauling equipment when the DJs played at parties. With time, I learnt how to work mixers and turntables and create my own samples. But my strength, they said, was in my playlists and how I arranged the songs. Within six months, I was making most of the mixtapes on cassettes and CDs for customers and even writing playlists for parties. It was years later before I would understand that I'd breached an impressive amount of copyright.

They said I always knew what people wanted to hear. Seyi, who loved words, called it a sentience; Onome called me a winsh (no matter how many times I pointed out that wizard was more appropriate in the circumstances); and Big S said it was a gift. But I couldn't take them seriously—after all, they believed New Edition was better after Bobby Brown left; plus, they never let me play at parties. When Big S had made the No Play Rule, he said it was because I was too young, and I needed to pass JAMB first. I'd begged him to let me play, even more passionately than the times I'd overheard my father begging our house-helps for sex. Now, after almost three years, hundreds of parties, and passing JAMB on my second attempt, I was yet to play.

"Talk to Big S for me. You've heard me lots of times. I'm ready. I can play blindfolded sef."

Seyi nodded. "I know. But this thing is bigger than Big S—shey you know?"

"How? What do you mean?"

But Seyi shook his head, put his earphones back on, and focused on the turntables. The conversation was over.

Sullen, I handed him a disc for the next song on the playlist—my playlist—A Tribe Called Quest's "Check the Rhime." Seyi shook his head again and reached instead for "Mind Playing Tricks on Me."

I loved how the Geto Boys seemed to speak to me in that song. I had it on repeat on my Walkman. But we had already played it at this party, and it wasn't yet time to repeat songs. So I rolled my eyes and shrugged my what-the-hell-are-you-doing at Seyi. He pointed at me.

Then I understood. The song was his gift to me—part apology, part encouragement.

So I did what anyone did with a gift. I accepted it.

"Your father packed out this afternoon. He has moved in with . . . with that shameless woman."

That was how my mother broke the news. Immediately, Chi Girl's face turned to a wet newspaper, crumpled and sodden. Majikpo already knew, so he sat puffed-up in what he mistook as the appropriate look for the new Man of the House. He looked constipated. It pried a smile from me. My grin, which was instinctive, was also because I was relieved—there'd be no more fighting and my having to break up fights, no more poison in the air, no more hiding in the music, and no more trying to manage the impossible feat of staying neutral in a war in which both sides demanded the demonization of the other.

As always, my mother misunderstood my smile.

"You are happy that your father is now with that witch, abi? You have sided with your father and that mami water against your own mother, abi?"

Pursed lips, angry finger pointing. "It had to be you. Foolish boy! You've always supported that useless man. Disciple! Oya, clap for yourself o! Clap!" She clapped for me. "You see yourself? I keep warning you—don't be like your father. But you've refused to hear word. Now you're just like him. Useless! Small JAMB, you can't even pass. Blockhead! Just like him."

If I'd wanted to nitpick, I'd have said many things. First, I would have said that I doubted if anyone could be a witch and a mami water at the same time. Then, I'd have reminded her that the JAMB aberration aside, I'd topped my class ninety percent of the time I'd been in school—it was one of the conditions for my being allowed to work at the Music Factory. Plus, I'd just passed JAMB, albeit on the second attempt. I'd have also said that, yes, although my father didn't discriminate in his compulsive womanising—he chased street hawkers with the same fervour as he did his female students—he was also a professor of applied physics at the Rivers State University. Certainly not a blockhead.

But I didn't nitpick.

I also wanted to explain to my mother that although I'd inherited my love and knowledge of music from my father, I was never going to be like him. I abhorred the idea of turning out any way like him. I didn't even look like him—it was Majikpo and Chi Girl who were his photocopies.

Perhaps it was a good thing I didn't say anything. Despite my best intentions, years later, I would eventually turn out like my father in many ways—the womanising and the self-inflicted mucking up of my marriage—but that's another story. My mother, in the midst of her madness, had prescience all those years when she warned me not to be like him. Like most mothers, she knew.

Later, during my nightly ritual of checking up on Chi Girl before she slept, she sat up in bed and asked a strange question. "I'm confused. Is Ms. Ukor a witch or a mermaid?"

I smiled. "She's none of them."

"Okay." But she didn't look convinced. "Okay, let me ask—is it better to be a witch or a mermaid?"

It was 1991. *The Little Mermaid*, her favourite movie at the time, had already been out for about two years. It had sold the fantasy of good mermaids. Maybe oyibo mermaids were good, but definitely not African ones despite Victor Uwaifo's song. African mermaids fucked up lives, spectacularly. Africans in the know, like our maternal grandfather who was a serious jazzman, were aware of this. He'd visited once when Chi Girl was watching *The Little Mermaid*. I could still hear his snorts of derision.

So, I said, "No one is better. If, God forbid, you see any of them, run. You hear me? Run." She nodded. I ruffled her hair and kissed her goodnight on her forehead.

Looking back, I can only add that I was glad *Harry Potter* hadn't yet been made.

My parents' room, now my mother's, was opposite Chi Girl's. I heard muffled sounds coming from behind the door. I rapped and opened the door without waiting for an answer.

My mother sat on the edge of the bed—on the side that used to be my father's. She squeezed the edge of the blanket as she sobbed into it. I crossed the room and knelt in front of her. On any other day, taking away the blanket and hugging my mother would have been awkward for both of us. But it was not any other day.

I held her. She clung to me. Her body trembled, wracked by the final and most painful heartbreak. And somewhere in all of it, it came to me suddenly. And I understood. I understood that despite fighting the man almost every day of her marriage, despite having to put up with his women and first-class bullshit, despite his lack of financial support and interest in his children, she loved him. God Almighty, she loved that man. And I remember thinking that if someone could ever love me with half of that, I'd have been blessed with something indescribably precious.

I held her till she ran out of her quota of tears for that day. Then I tucked her in bed, still on his side. I knelt there, still holding her. I only let her go when sleep showed mercy and took her away. Before leaving the room and turning off the light, I kissed her forehead. It was the last time I'd kiss my mother.

Somehow, after everything that happened that day, I never got around to asking my mother why she had instructed Big S not to let me play at parties.

The next time I saw Prof was about four months later at a party.

I'd taken to calling my father Prof sometime after he left the house. Till today, I'm not sure why.

When Big S had told me the party was a joint one for the alumni of some American Ivy League who finished in the sixties and seventies, I suspected he'd be there. The party was held outdoors in one of those old colonial-style mansions in Old GRA on its sprawling lawn, which was lush, green, and smooth as a pool table. I didn't see him when he came in. Big S, who was playing, nudged me. I looked up. He pointed at Prof with his chin.

I raised my eyes, saw Ms. Ukor for the first time, and the world stopped.

Just like that.

She was startlingly beautiful in a way that made you want to go down on your knees in worship. Her face—knowing and twinkling in eyes, high in forehead and cheekbones, delicious, pouty, and soft red in lips—burned holes in the brain, making her unforgettable. She was fair, a light caramel, and she walked with the gracious ease of royalty. Prof was beside her. As he strolled with a triumphant swagger, he took many long pauses to shake every man's hand while really showing her off.

I'd heard a lot about her—how treacherous she was, how she was unmarriageable, preferring instead to be a professional husband-snatcher, and how she was really in her mid-forties even though she looked thirty-something (my mother was wrong—she looked twenty-eight at most). And my first thought, when my brain started to thaw, was, *Fashi all you heard. This woman too fine!* Then I looked at Prof's glowing face, and I knew I couldn't begrudge him his happiness with this woman. Plus, I would be a hypocrite to judge him when I'd have run away with her. (I was still naïve then; life would later teach me that sometimes it was okay to be a hypocrite.)

Big S was smitten too. "Your father is a correct guy. Kai! That woman fine."

I nodded and smiled.

The music wasn't too loud because it was a party for middle-aged people—they needed to hear themselves talk. Big S played his playlist of mid-tempo hits of the time for a while—Color Me Badd's "I Wanna Sex You Up," "I Can't Wait Another Minute" from Hi-Five, and Aaron Neville's "Everybody Plays the Fool." A few heads nodded, some feet tapped, but nobody danced. We were both experienced enough to know they weren't really feeling the music.

Prof and Ms. Ukor sat and sipped bright umbrellaed drinks round a garden table under the shade of a giant umbrella.

"Let me go greet him," I said.

Big S's grin was sarcastic—*yeah right.*

Prof beamed when he saw me. He got up and gave me a hug as tight and as warm as the one that the rich man gave his prodigal son. Nobody watching us would have guessed that I'd gone to his office several times over the past month to request money for school (I'd just gained admission into UniPort), but he had refused to see me each time. Maybe that was why I started calling him Prof.

He did the introductions. "This is Iverem Ukor. And this is my second and favourite son, Tukwashi."

"G-g-g . . . good evening." My voice sounded like it belonged to someone else.

She flicked her wrist—a short wave. But her smile gave my heart a sweet and violent kick.

It was Prof's turn to stammer. "Erm, erm, Ms. Ukor is an alumna of MIT, just like me, though she graduated twelve years later." His smile was nervous. "It was a wonderful coincidence that we would meet as lecturers in this university."

I smiled politely but thought, *But it's no coincidence that you're now screwing, is it?*

After a moment of uncomfortable silence, she asked, "Aren't you the one who's in a band or something?"

And just like that, the spell was broken. Her voice was high-pitched, nasal, whiny. Hearing her felt like someone was shredding my mind with a grater. As if that wasn't bad enough, she spoke with a fake American accent. Two of my pet peeves.

"No, I'm a DJ."

"Oh, that's nice." She nodded towards the direction of Big S. "So, you're with him?"

"Yes, that's my boss."

She lowered her voice to a conspiratorial whisper even though Big S was too far away to hear. "Well then, perhaps you can play something that will wake up this party?"

I shook my head. "I can't play, but I'll pass on the message."

A perfect eyebrow arched in query. "What do you mean you can't play?"

I shrugged.

Then I turned to Prof. It was bare-knuckle boxing time. I said, "I need money. I'm starting school next week."

His smile was tight, uncomfortable. "Come to the office. We'll talk there."

"No. I'll take a cheque now."

Like the afterthought it was, I added, "Please."

Prof always went around with his cheque book. We both knew this. We stared at each other till he gave up. He sighed and pulled out the cheque book from the inside pocket of his jacket. "How much do you need?"

I told him.

"Ahn-ahn! That's too much na."

"Oh c'mon, Ameh. Give the boy what he wants."

My father's first name is Amezhi. Till today, I can't explain why I felt she had diminished him, the legendary Prof Amezhi Thomas, by shortening his name to Ameh. Maybe it was her annoying voice. Maybe it was the irritation in her tone. Or maybe it was because I wasn't used to him being scorned by any other woman except my mother. (And at that moment, I remembered my mother and how she still cried every night, now behind her locked door.) Whatever it was, it started my irrational loathing for Ms. Ukor.

We didn't know it then, but eventually, Prof would stay true to his nature and leave Ms. Ukor for a nurse who worked at the Staff Clinic. And Ms. Ukor, according to the gossip, would remain bewildered, especially because, in her words, the nurse was gorilla ugly. And I would laugh when the story reached me and forever add nurses to my list of favourite people. It would be years later before I realised how much my dislike for Ms. Ukor (and my fear of being like Prof) would screw up my mind. Because they reminded me of her, I would never date slim, light-skinned women—well, except Arese, but that's another story.

I went back to Big S with the cheque burning in my pocket. There was also a buzz in my head. It felt hallucinogenic, and maybe that was what pushed me, without any forethought, to do what happened next.

"She says hi. Also, she says you should let me play. She says you should do it as a favour to her."

His forehead furrowed into a suspicious frown.

I shrugged. "You can go and ask her if you want. Oh look! She's looking at us. No slacking. Wave now."

We waved. Big S moved his hand mechanically as if he were in a daze. She waved back. His jaw slacked open. Gambler on a roll, I'd pushed my luck one more time, and it was still good.

What happened next would make Big S continue to believe that I have a gift for knowing exactly what people want to hear. I didn't think it was a gift. I just knew music and could read people better than most. A party of middle-aged and middle-class Nigerians who schooled in Ivy League America in the sixties and seventies, wanted to relive their youth, and were wannabe Americans at heart would not be swayed by the pop and hip-hop hits of 1991. No sir. They would only move to soul and funk and disco and Motown—they were the *Soul Train* generation.

So I made a quick playlist. Nothing on paper. It was all in my head. I had to fill the floor quickly, so the dance songs came first—"I Want You Back" by the Jackson 5, "What'd I Say" by Ray Charles, "Got to Give It Up (Part 1)" by Marvin Gaye, Stevie Wonder's "Signed, Sealed, Delivered, I'm Yours," "Respect" by Aretha Franklin; I even threw in "Da Ya Think I'm Sexy" by Rod Stewart. The playlist was sixty-three songs long. But till today, I can remember every song on it. I've played them a thousand times in my head.

But before I started, something happened. Big S announced me. "Ladies and gentlemen, he's about to burn these wheels of steel. He's the new Big Deal. Let's give it up for DJ TT!"

TT were the initials of my name—Tukwashi Thomas. Now, I know it was a crappy stage name, but in my defence, I was seventeen years old. Everyone did regrettable shit at seventeen.

Apart from Ms. Ukor, who clapped politely, everybody ignored my introduction. I didn't care. I knew I was going to be their Pied Piper—I was going to make them dance for as long as

I pleased. Big S stepped from behind the turntables and waved me in. He gently took off the headphones from behind his head with both hands. Still with both hands, he put them on me as I lowered my head for my coronation.

The first thing I did was cut the music. It got everyone's attention. They looked at me. I put my first song on. It was on vinyl—"Stayin' Alive" by the Bee Gees. They heard that unmistakable beat, screamed, and began rushing to the dance floor. I waited for exactly eleven seconds and scratched it to a teasing stop. They groaned. I smiled.

Then I lifted my fingers and let the music play.

"Hurt"*

Your mother starts crying when Dami turns up for his funeral. He is fashionably late. You expect this. You also expect him to overdo his entrance, but you are still surprised by what he comes up with. First, he appears from a chauffeur-driven Bentley Mulsanne. (You have no idea where he rented or borrowed it from.) Then, a red carpet is actually rolled out for him. He completes the show with a tailored tuxedo and Aviator sunglasses even though it's past six p.m., and it has been dark and drizzling all day. He waves to family and friends under canopies on the family house's front lawn. They chortle and applaud. It causes him to break character, and his smug facade slips into laughter. Chuckling, your mother starts shaking her head, but she's still crying. Then in a blink, she's out of the blocks to him. She wraps her arms round his midriff, hangs on tight, and chants his name like a prayer. "Damiete. Damiete. Damiete."

When your mother finally releases him, he gives a warm hug to Ejeme, your wife. Then he sees you, smiles, and tries to do his usual

* Written under the influence of "Hurt" cover by Johnny Cash

strut, but it's one-sided and leaden. He reaches you and opens his arms, inviting you to check him out. "You like?"

You think bow ties are silly, but Dami easily pulled off wearing a black one, even now. You straighten it. You hug him, tentatively, because you're mindful of his dapper baffs, how much weight he has lost, how fragile he looks, and because you remember yesterday's conversation with Joy.

Then you remember the last time you saw him with a bow tie. It was the day of his confirmation at St. Cyprian's in '93, which was, coincidentally, also his thirteenth birthday. It was a white clip-on—he was dressed in all white, a cherub on his last day of innocence—and you, his eighteen-year-old brother, had playfully pulled his cheeks as you fixed the tie. Kalada had been there too, aloof and scowling because those were the only ways he knew to show that he was the first son, and he was too cool for church. Dami squeezes you, and you know he remembers that day. You squeeze too. Then you step back, dust imaginary fluff off his shoulders, tug the tie again, and nod your approval. "Fine boy! Nothing do you."

But something is doing Dami. It's eating him sef. Brain tumour. Malignant. Stage 4. Inoperable. Discovered too late to treat. You had insisted that he treat it anyway. But all the radiotherapy did was to tire him out, make him vomit, and thin his hair. When he stopped it, his new hair grew so freakishly curly that you yabbed him about his Jheri curls. He couldn't do much about the mood swings and the growing paralysis on his left side. But he could do painkillers for the persistent headaches, and as you expected, he overdosed them to the point where he was almost always higher than God's kite. When you talked about it, he had laughed, pointed out that it was a peaceful, calming high, and told you to be grateful that he was no longer on his usual psychotic trips from his "recreational stimulants." His quip made you search his room for illegal opioids—he had moved from the family house into the guest bedroom of your house—and he, smirking all through, waited for you to finish the search before telling you he had been clean for months. But knowing Dami, it was safer not to believe him.

The most optimistic doctors had given him five months to live. He was down to the last four weeks. And because Dami never did things like normal people, he had insisted on organising and attending his funeral. "It's going to be the best funeral ever," he promised. "People are going to wish they were dead so they can have a funeral like mine." And he laughed, and you chuckled because you understood. And Ejeme, who didn't understand yet, had assumed the laughter meant Dami was joking as he always did—until the day she saw you making online transfers to pay the caterers and decorators. You tried to explain. You told her about Kalada and your father, but your words came out in weak trickles like a drying tap, and you knew she still didn't understand. So she asked Dami, and all he did was smile his lopsided smile and say, "You know all those things you are going to say about me when I die? I'm throwing my funeral so you can tell me yourself."

Your mother hadn't taken the news of Dami's funeral well. "Over my dead body!" she had declared. The added insult was that it was to be held in the family house where she lived. Somehow, she managed to blame you for it. And when she realised you were funding the funeral, she accused you, in typical Nigerian mother hyperbole, of conspiring with Dami to kill her before her time. But whenever she spoke to Dami, as expected, she never talked to him about it or forbade him from having the funeral. She'd only sob and promise him that he was going to bury her and not the other way around. But Dami would smile and casually say something cruel, like tell her not to die before him because he didn't have money to bury her. And she'd wail some more. And Dami would pretend to fall asleep till she left, or he'd call in your twin three-year-old daughters to entertain him while he ignored her. It was always uncomfortable for you to watch your mother suffer for her favourite and last child. But you were too jaded to intervene.

Dami clasps your shoulders and leans in as though he wants to hug you again. He whispers, "How was your Lagos trip?"

You whisper back. "Rough. Just got back this afternoon. Oil prices are still dropping. I couldn't get them to reverse the slashing of our contracts and . . ." You stop because you realise that's not what he wants to know.

He speaks more plainly. "You saw Joy?"

"Yes. Yesterday evening."

"Did you convince her to come?"

You pause. Then you lie. "I don't know."

He sighs. His shoulders slump.

You lie again. "Hey, she may turn up. The night is still young." You slap his cheek playfully. "Chin up. It's your night. We're waiting for you to start the show."

Dami had been calling it a living funeral; the banners declared it a "Celebration of the Life of Damiete Kuruye-Briggs"; your mother was expecting it to be more of a service of songs, a sombre event. But you knew, and Dami knew you knew that whatever it was when it started, last-last, it must turn into a roaring party.

He boom-laughs. "The show must go on, abi?"

You nod.

He resets his sunglasses. "Okay na. Let's give them a show."

"I hear Dami is dying. Is it true?"

"Yes."

"What's wrong with him?"

You told her.

"Is he in pain?"

"Plenty."

Joy smiled. "That's good."

Expecting a reaction, she stared hard at you. You didn't give her one. Or rather, you didn't give her the one she hoped for. Experience from negotiating many oil service contracts meant you were expert in masking your surprise. You used your fork to move the asun and pepper on your plate around. You asked, "Are you sure you don't want to eat something?"

"I'm sure."

"Something to drink?"

"I've said I don't want anything."

It was day four of your five-day trip to Lagos. You had called Joy before you left Port Harcourt, as soon as you landed in Lagos, and every day, hoping to meet with her. She had posted you and posted you, but eventually, she agreed to dinner. She met you at the rooftop balcony restaurant of your hotel. It was the first time you were seeing her in almost four years. She was still svelte and stylish, but you were shocked by how much verve had been drained from her, leaving behind a doll-like shell.

"I'm so sorry, Priye. I shouldn't have talked to you like that."

You shrugged. "It's okay." You placed the cutlery on the plate. "I'll get to the point. I'm in Lagos for some business. Dami asked me to use the chance to see you and apologise on his behalf. He says he's sorry for everything. He says he can't apologise himself because you don't take his calls and refuse to see him anytime he comes to Lagos." You reached into your jacket and pulled out the envelope containing Dami's letter. You slid it across the table. "He also said I should give this to you."

Joy didn't touch it or look at it.

"He's having a living funeral tomorrow evening. I know it's short notice, but he wants you to attend. I also want you to. If you prefer, I'll cover all costs: airfares, hotel, everything—"

"I don't want your money!" She shook her head vehemently. "And I'm definitely not going." Almost immediately, she raised a hand in apology for her tone. You smiled.

"Why is he having a living funeral?"

You shrugged. "You know Dami always wants to stand out."

You don't tell her that though you were both Kalabari men, Dami hated Kalabari funerals. You had both attended two, both of which cut deeply.

The first was for Kalada. Deceived by his natural strong head, he joined a university confra and formed gangster even though he was a middle-class kid who grew up in GRA in Port Harcourt. One night, he was cornered by a rival gang in his room in Choba, off-campus in UniPort, and shot as he pleaded for his life. He was buried in Abonnema, your ancestral town. Until the last year of his life when he joined confra, you had all been closely knit, especially both of you, as he was only two years older. Dami was thirteen when Kalada died. You and Dami would have preferred to mourn Kalada quietly, but Kalabari funerals, like most African funerals, didn't create room for private grief. So, you and Dami endured the pawing crowds, the strangers who forced their familiarity on you because they were distant relatives, and the rites you thought were ridiculous. And in the middle of the all-night din koru, Dami had suddenly turned to you and whispered, "I'd rather die than be buried like a Kalabari man." And you were so surprised that you laughed. And your father and some of his fellow chiefs frowned, and someone told you off for your indecorum.

Your father died two years after Kalada. The stroke that killed him came with a black sense of humour: it caught him in his mistress's house, some say in the middle of sex, others say in the middle of a meal; either way, it caught him sha. Because he was a prominent chief, his was the society wedding of funerals. After the frills—renovation of the family house in Abonnema prior to the burial, mortuary fees for ten months, the gun and cannon salutes that were enough to fight a small war, the lavish canoe regattas, the drums and masquerades, three ornate lying-in-state beds—his oil-tools supplying company was in debt.

But the bigger loss was watching them gradually demean your mother. And when they came to shave your mother's hair as required by tradition, you and Dami grabbed machetes and dared them to touch her. She pleaded with you to let them, and you refused. The standoff only ended when she took the scissors and calmly hacked her hair in ugly haphazard patterns, and Dami's tears flowed like they would never stop. And during her one-year post-funeral confinement (she was to stay shaven, wear black daily, and not leave the family house in Port Harcourt during the period), on many nights, she allowed you to sneak her out and drive her around the city while she stared out the window in silence. Sometimes Dami joined you, and on those nights, with the roads free of traffic and your mother watching quietly from the back seat, you taught your baby brother how to drive.

You tuned out your memories and refocused on Joy. "If tomorrow's short notice, come sometime soon. He needs to see you." Maybe the reminiscing made you maudlin because you did something you wouldn't normally do—you begged. "Please reconsider. Please," you said. "I'm not asking you to come see Dami because you were married to him . . . well technically, the divorce hasn't been finalised yet. I'm asking because you were both in love once, and I'm hoping that a part of that love, even if it's just a tiny part, is still alive."

"Fuck love!"

It came out sharp, loud, like a slap. It startled people at nearby tables, and they looked at you, some sniggering. You stared them down till they looked away. You turned to Joy and noticed she was trembling from all the effort of trying to control her anger.

She spoke in a clipped, biting whisper. "And tell me, Priye—did you preach this love to Dami when he was beating me?"

"Dami beat you?" Your voice was a weak croak.

"Like a slave. Almost every day for three years." She paused when she read your face. "Wait . . . you didn't know?"

"I had no idea. I'm so sorry." After a long, awkward pause, you say, "Please . . . tell me about it . . . if you can."

She exhaled, and it seemed to bleed out some of the anger. "Apart from the time he kicked me till I had a miscarriage, or the three times he cracked my ribs, or the bruises, scratches, and broken teeth, there isn't much to tell." As she talked, she pulled her phone from her handbag and poked it till she found what she wanted. "There are plenty of pictures though." She turned the phone's screen to you. There was a picture on it. At first glance, it looked like a piece of fresh bloodied meat. Then you realised it was her face. She offered the phone. "Just swipe. There's a whole folder full of these."

You swiped. Two pictures in and you almost stopped. You managed to get to the end of the folder and handed the phone to her. The pictures had scattered your head. So, you put your head in your hands and tried to nurse it. When you let go, a weariness had crept up and smothered your soul. You hadn't planned to drink, but you signalled a waiter and ordered a rum and Coke. That was when Joy ordered a vodka. You both were quiet till the drinks came and the first gulps went down.

"I'm so sorry. I wish you had told me then. I'd have stopped it."

She shrugged. "At the time, you and Dami weren't talking. I told your mother sha. I assumed she told you."

"My mother?" You chuckled, but there was no mirth in it. "She would never tell me when Dami screws up."

After your father's death, perhaps to compensate for something you would never understand, your mother overpampered Dami. Despite your constant protests, she changed his wardrobe twice a year, paid for his regular parties, got him a car when he finally passed JAMB on his third attempt, and indulged his every outlandish whim. This was at a time when your father's company, which funded your family, was struggling to pay salaries and stay in business. Maybe that contributed to Dami growing into a lazy, entitled man. You took over the running of the company in Dami's second year at UniLag. At the end of his third year, he decided, suddenly, that he'd drop out and go to school in the UK, and he demanded that the company pay for this. You refused at first, preferring that he finished his last year and go for a master's instead, but your mother nagged you ragged. Finally, after cutting the company's costs by laying off four employees, men with families, you raised the funds for Dami. In his ten years in the UK before he was deported, all he managed to do was drop out of two universities and gain a drug habit. And all that time, the company, which you had stabilised and grown, paid his bills.

On his return, your mother insisted that you appoint him as a director in the company. Reluctantly, you did, and Dami surprised you. He worked hard, restricted his partying to weekends, married Joy, and seemed to have gotten his shit together. He did all this for one year, till the day he forged your signature on cheques and other authorisations and cleaned out just over one hundred ninety-six million from the company's main operating account. He refused to return the money. Your mother forbade you from having him arrested. You filed a civil lawsuit. He fled to Lagos with Joy. Your mother eventually got you to drop the lawsuit. But for four years, she was unable to get you and Dami talking again—until the tumour.

Joy sighed. "I'm sorry to say this, but . . ." She didn't sound sorry. "Your mother made Dami the asshole he is. You know that, right?"

You thought about it for a moment. "She enabled him, yes. But he was destined to be an asshole."

It forced a reluctant smile from her and broke some of the remaining tension.

"I'm really sorry."

"It's okay. It's not your fault." She leaned back with a wistful look in her eye. "You know, it wasn't the beatings that made me leave him. It was the STDs." She sighed. "I still can't believe I was that stupid. Looking back, I could have easily killed him. . . ." She sighed again and stared at you without blinking. "I wish I had. All those years, I could have slipped something in his food or cut off his penis as he slept."

You chuckled.

"Why are you laughing?"

You could have told her you have a quirk that makes you laugh at inappropriate moments. Instead, you just shook your head and said, "It's nothing. Forget about it."

You took advantage of another lengthy silence to finish your drink. You caught her eyes, held them, and said as honestly as you could, "I hope you forgive yourself and you heal fully soon."

Her smile was sad. "I'm glad you didn't say I should forgive him."

You shrugged. "I suspect that comes as part of the full healing package."

"I'll heal when I see Dami's grave. I plan to spit on it."

"That's not going to happen."

Her eyes flashed. "Is that a dare?"

"You don't understand." You exhaled. "He wants to be cremated."

"She didn't come."

It had been a good, fun night. Despite how weak he was, Dami had played his best public Dami—cracking jokes, telling the tallest of tales, charming and yabbing everyone, shining in the limelight, a dying star in its supernova. And while there was an underlying sadness to his last performance, surprisingly, it was without any self-pity. You lost count of the number of people who said they wanted a living funeral or would consider one.

Dami repeats himself. "Joy didn't come."

You don't reply. You focus on propping his pillows and settling him, half-sitting in them, the way he likes. You'd developed a ritual of visiting him late at night after your twins, Ejeme, and Dami's full-time live-in nurse had turned in. You'd give him any remaining medication, prop his pillows, sit on the chair beside his bed, watch TV, and chill till he fell asleep. Sometimes, there are conversations. Mostly, it's about old times, when you were kids, when your father and Kalada were still around; sometimes it's about the now, your kids, how he is coping with his illness. But Dami never talks about his hedonistic years in the UK or about the one year he worked for the company upon his return. And you never talk about the money he took.

He watches you for a while and then says, "You knew she wasn't going to come, didn't you?"

This is the moment to give him a good talking to. You want to yell and tell him that of all his screw-ups in life, beating Joy was the one you were most disappointed about. But you just say, "After all you did, do you blame her?"

His smile is tight. "Yeah, I don't blame her."

For a long moment, you both blankly stare at the TV. Then he sighs heavily. "I was tripped out of my mind almost all the time. It doesn't justify it, but . . ." He tries to flick a wrist to push his point across, but his hand drops down weakly. "I've been trying to stop being that man." He sighs again and smiles. "It seems I've run out of time and chances to make things right." He turns away, but you manage to catch the end of his momentary wince. And you understand that his pain is not only physical.

You face the TV and allow yourself to be lost in its mindlessness. When you turn to Dami, he's asleep, chin on chest, snoring lightly. You mute the TV, but you don't turn it off—Dami prefers sleeping with the TV on. You pull the blanket over him, and he doesn't stir. You turn off the lights and walk to the door.

"Priye . . ."

"Yes?"

"Did I ever apologise to you for . . . for everything?"

It takes a little while before you answer. "No."

From the light of the TV, you can see that Dami has this big shit-eating grin. "Don't worry. One day, I will."

You both start laughing.

Your secretary shows Joy into your office, and you come from behind your desk. You are not sure how to greet her. You're pleasantly surprised when she gives you a hug—an awkward, stiff, half hug, but technically, still a hug. You lead her to the visitors' sofa in a corner of the office. She asks for water. You ask your secretary to get some. You only knew she was in Port Harcourt when she called you on her way from the airport. You tell her to give you some notice next time so you can pick her up from the airport or send a car for her. She shrugs, and you can't tell what that means. Your secretary brings the water and leaves. She ignores the water. She asks if she can look at the pictures on the shelf behind your desk. She doesn't wait for your reply before she looks. There are four pictures: one of Ejeme, one of your girls, and one of your sideburned father in an eighties-style suit, writing with one hand and the receiver of a rotary dial phone in his ear while sitting in this same office.

The final picture was taken when you were ten to mark your father's chieftaincy. You and Kalada stood behind your sitting parents; Dami was between them, smiling through one missing milk tooth and holding your father's gold walking stick. Your father was in his opulent ceremonial don and was crowned with an attigra that had small mirrors and a plume of purple and yellow feathers; your mother wore her chunky coral beads and a kilali headgear; and you boys wore white etibos and bowler hats. Joy stares at this picture for a long time, an indecipherable look on her face.

She speaks without turning to you. "Why did you cremate him in Lagos?"

"There's no crematorium in Port Harcourt."

She turns to you. "I couldn't come." It was almost an apology.

"I understand."

You had called her when Dami died, before the reading of the will and just before the cremation. Although she had passed on her perfunctory condolences to you and your mother on the phone, she hadn't visited—till now, ten months later.

"You have to stop paying money into my account."

You shake your head. "I can't. He left his shares in the company to you."

She looks at you suspiciously. "What kind of company pays dividends every month?"

You smile. "I've not paid you his dividends yet—that will come at the end of the year. I'm just paying you his post-death benefits based on his contract as a director of the company. You're his named beneficiary."

"But you removed him as a director years ago."

"I reappointed him a week before he passed."

She closes her eyes and rubs her temple. "Why are you doing this?"

"Because that's what he wanted . . . it's what we both want."

She hisses. "He thought he could buy me?"

"No. I'm the one trying to buy . . ." You shake your head. "I don't know what I'm trying to buy sef. The past, maybe? Penance?"

"I don't understand."

It takes awhile before you answer. Although your emotions are this deep whirlpool, you know it will barely produce enough words to explain the turmoil in your soul whenever you remember Dami. You try anyway.

"Dami was a bad man, but he was also my baby brother. That means it was my responsibility to smack him when he was bad but not hard enough to kill him. So he stole millions from the company. I smacked and he ran, right? Guess what? Everything he took, I made it back in two years. I knew the right people, oil prices were good, everyone was drilling. Two years! But I didn't talk to him for four."

You pause and sigh. "In those four years, I got married and didn't invite him. In those four years, a tumour began to grow in his head. And because he had blown all the money and couldn't afford treatment, and because we weren't talking, it grew into a monster. By the time I heard, it was too late."

Your voice starts cracking. "I threw money at that tumour, trying to buy my brother's life. The same bloody money that made me not talk to him for four years. But the tumour didn't want money. All it wanted was to eat my brother. I threw money at my brother. Whatever he wanted to do with it—steal it, smoke it—I didn't care. But by then, all he really wanted was to stay with me. Make up for the lost years. Get to know my family. Play with my kids. Curl up and die in peace in my house." You exhale. "So, I'm the one doing all the buying here."

You turn away, pretending not to see the tears in her eyes. Then she says, "I'm sorry you lost your brother." She adds hesitantly, "And I really mean it."

You don't know what to say, so you nod and change the topic. "And you? Hope you've healed."

She fidgets for a moment. "I'm not there yet, but I'm getting better."

You nod again. "Take your time."

Then she smiles, part tentative, part mischievous. "You too. Heal soon."

"Song for Someone"*

You are waiting for one man. But you're exchanging glances and half smiles with another man, bald, who sits alone in a corner.

A third man, a stranger, walks to you, stands over your table, and offers to buy you a drink. T-Pain.

Your teacup is halfway up when he speaks. You pause for a second, then glance at the stranger as you sip. When you reunite the cup with its matching saucer, you say, "No, thank you." You flash a smile, which you hope is polite, non-bitchy, but also non-flirty (this is important). Also, you smile because you want to let him down gently without bruising his ego in front of his friends—you'd noticed he'd come from a table where two other men still sat, drinking and watching both of you.

The man pulls the chair opposite you and sits. His perfume, some expensive oud that he has overdosed on, chokes you, killing the soothing scent of the ginger tea you'd been drinking in. He casually drops his car key fob and phone on the table, but they're

* Written under the influence of "Song for Someone" by U2

strategically placed for you to notice he drives a Mercedes-Benz and has an iPhone XS. "I hope you don't mind."

"I do, actually. I'm waiting for someone."

He leers like you just told him you wanted to blow him. He has the air of a man who expects everybody to be as enamoured with his good looks as he is. He puts his elbows on the table and clasps one of his fists in the other. "You remind me of . . ."

You don't hear the rest because you think, *Usher*. And you do a quick scan of his songs in your mind's jukebox, select "U Remind Me," and start singing in your head. It's something you do—remember songs and lyrics when people talk, and sing in your head while tuning out people you don't want to talk to. You are in the middle of the second verse when you realise he's stopped talking. You cut the music and stare at him like, *What?*

"You're not paying attention," he scolds.

Now you want to roll your eyes, hard enough to dislocate them. Instead, you say, "Please, if you don't mind, I'd like to be left alone." Your tone is even, respectful even, and low enough so it doesn't carry beyond your table to within earshot of the other people in the almost-empty restaurant-bar of the Golf Club. The bald man watches intently from his corner.

"You should be nice to me. I can take care of you."

You massage your temples gently while doing a slow headshake. You close your eyes for a moment.

"Look, Kel . . ."

You open your eyes because he calls your name, or rather a shortened form of your name.

"My name is Ukela." There's a hardness in your voice.

He shrugs. "Whatever." Then he leans forward and half shuts his lids, making his eyes bedroomy and dreamy. "I want you," he drawls. "Let's stop playing games. I'm rich. And I know what you are." He half puckers, then licks his lips like LL Cool J. "I'm willing to pay whatever you want. How much?"

Things have happened to you when you waited for men.

Like the time, seven years ago, with Victor.

You were alone at a table near the poolside of Blue Elephant waiting for Victor, your fiancé. He was running late, but you'd ordered the grilled prawns and fries for him because that was what he always ate at that restaurant. You weren't hungry, and you nursed a Sprite to pass the time.

It was dusk. Thursday. 10th March 2011. You remember the date because your traditional wedding was scheduled for Saturday that week and the church wedding for the next Saturday. You were twenty-six.

You glanced up from your phone and saw Victor striding towards you, fast. You'd started smiling at him when you glimpsed Anele, his best friend, anxious, running to catch up with him. But he didn't catch Victor before Victor reached you.

Actually, Victor's roar of "Slut!" reached you first. A half second later, his big right hand slap-grabbed your throat, and half lifted you from the seat. His face was twisted into a snarl as he repeated his greeting. "Ashawo!"

You'd met Victor when he gave you a job in his architecture firm just after you got your MArch. He was a sweet, gentle man with a booming laugh that bounced off walls and shook everywhere he went because he laughed often. He was smitten by you. It took one week for him to shed his pretence of professionalism and ask you on a date. You turned him down. But he was persistent, pleasantly so, without pestering you. And he was genuinely a prince of a boss, loved by everyone in the small firm. After three months of late-night working after midnight, firm-wide akara or cupcakes for breakfast, helping you get better at modifying construction plans on CAD, all punctuated with mild teasing and mutual laughter, you agreed to have drinks with him. You ended up at his flat. The sex was tolerable, and he fell fast—asleep and for you. In a week, he declared his undying love. In a month, he'd proposed—a choreographed and cloying public exhibition that came with the kneeling, cameras, and an expectant audience of strangers, as standard. You couldn't say no.

"You fucked Opus yesterday?" Victor asked as he clamped your throat with one hand.

"Leave her. Release her, abeg," Anele pleaded.

He grimaced and squeezed. "Answer me!"

But you couldn't talk. Your hands tried, feebly, to unclasp Victor's fingers while your legs thrashed uselessly.

"Guy, you're choking her. Leave her."

Victor finally listened and drop-shoved you awkwardly on the armrest of the chair. Your weight toppled the chair, and you sprawled on the floor. You looked up to see people recording with their phones and Victor towering over you.

"You and Opus. Start talking."

You started scream-crying instead. Between body-racking sobs and streaming tears while rubbing your throat, you managed to blurt, "How could you? How dare you assault me? You attacked me based on a lie and—"

"A lie?"

"Yes, a filthy lie from the pit of hell!" Your words were amped by the appropriate doses of vehemence and righteous indignation. "There's nothing between Opus and me."

Victor nodded slowly, but his smile was bitter. He pulled his phone from his pocket, scrolled through it for a moment, and turned the screen to you. It was a video.

Later, people would say Opunabo, or Opus, the hedonistic maritime magnate, was your sugar daddy because he was older and wealthier. It wasn't that simple. Before Victor, you'd been on and off with Opus. It was a situationship, never quite switched on or off. It worked for both of you because there were no obligations or demands; and the sex, fuelled by Viagra and MDMA, was mind-bending. Opus was fanatical about sex tapes. There were several tapes of both of you, but they were always with your consent, or so you believed. Yesterday, you'd honoured his request to see him "for the last time before the wedding." Looking back, the only sign he'd given that he was resentful about the wedding was when, in the middle of pulling down your skirt, he offered to pay you to call it off. It had been so unexpected and odd that you laughed it off as a joke, and he chuckled too. He'd sent the recording to Victor a few minutes before he arrived at Blue Elephant.

You turned your eyes from the video, but the sounds of you moaning and talking dirty filled the air. You'd never talked dirty to Victor. Anele snatched the phone from Victor's hand and stopped the video.

Silence.

There you were, still on the floor, skirt rode up your thighs. There he was, his spirit crushed, his face wet with tears. The moment was long and hopeless, a preview of some eternal damnation.

"I'm sorry, Victor." That was all you could manage.

"Why?" His voice went soft, the Victor you knew.

You sighed. "Because this is who I am."

You say, "Keep your money. Say something intelligent."

It confuses the man. "What?"

"You said you're willing to pay whatever I want so you can sleep with me, right? Well, I'm saying, keep your money, say something intelligent instead, and I'll do you for free."

He looks at you like you're crazy. You look at him like he's an olodo, till gradually, the smugness drains from his face.

You raise an eyebrow. "I'm waiting."

He opens his mouth, but apart from some "erms" and two false starts, no words come out.

"Oga, please show me that you have some sense. Small sense sef." Your voice is now deliberately loud. It startles him, so as he jerks back, he mistakenly hits the table, juddering your saucer, his phone and car key fob. Everybody in the restaurant turns and stares.

You rescue the teacup, bring it close to your face, and glance at him over the rim. "You do realise that your money can't cure your stupidity, right?"

Like slow-twisted metal, his beautiful face contorts into a murderous frown.

"Eh-yah, fine man like you, but you're a blockhead." You tsk-tsk. "Tragic. Tragic."

He mutters, "Bitch."

"Same to you, my sister."

The man stands up quickly, grabbing his things. He glares at you for a long moment while you smirk. Then, perhaps he realises that no matter how far this went today, you'd always get the last word, and each time would be more caustic than the last. Eventually, he trudges the walk of shame back to his friends. You hide your chuckle behind your teacup. The bald man in the corner smiles and looks away.

That's when the man you're waiting for walks in.

The last time you saw him was three years ago, and now he's all grey, coiffed hair and beard. He is a tall man, and his shoulders are beginning to stoop, but his eyes still twinkle, and his charm still works. You know this because before he makes his way to you, people go up to him to shake his hand, pay obeisance, and laugh uproariously at his quips. They know him here. They probably know him everywhere.

Eventually, he's in front of you. You stand and hug him. It's a warm, fierce thing, and his hug back is tentative at first before he clings to you and breathes in your hair. When you unclinch, his brow is still up in pleasant surprise. You shrug and smile like, *Ehn-hen, I hugged you tight. So what?*

A waiter pulls a chair for him. Before he sits, he leans his gold-knobbed walking stick beside the chair. He sits, smoothens an imaginary crease on his impeccably styled etibo, and steeples his fingers, showing off his gold—ornate cufflinks, watch, signet ring on his left pinky—and red chieftaincy beads on his right wrist. He searches your face and says, "Hello, Prodigal."

"Hello, BB." His name is Chief Buduma Benson, but everyone calls him BB.

He sighs. "I prefer you call me Dad or Father."

"Okay, BB."

You both laugh.

He notices the waiter ready to take orders. He asks, "You want something to drink?"

You shake your head. "Not really." You turn to the waiter. "Just some more hot water please."

"Hot water?"

"For ginger tea. I carry a box in my handbag."

He makes a sour face. "It sounds abominable."

You shrug. "That's your wahala. Me, I like it."

He nods to the waiter. "Hot water for my daughter. The usual for me." The man bows and disappears. You unabashedly study each other for a long while. Then he muses, "You know, among all my children, you look like me the most. Really fascinating."

"Typical. It's God's favourite trick to play on fathers who have bastard children." You smile. "I like God's sense of humour."

His smile is rueful. "You're not a bastard. And I always provided for you."

You shrug. "True. But some things were more important than money."

Your parents met when your mother was BB's secretary in his construction company. At the time, he was already married and the father of three boys. When your mother got pregnant with you, she went on maternity leave and never returned to work even after you were born. She didn't have to. BB was the type of man who put his mistress's allowances and living expenses on his company's tab. But it came at a cost—she was to keep herself and you away from any spotlight. This meant that though you shared the same surname, you had to be guarded about your father's identity in primary and secondary school. Looking back, it wasn't hard to do because he was a phantom, ghosting in and out your mother's flat in Elekahia Estate at night when you were already in bed or sleeping. And there were no pictures of him in the flat. The first time you remembered studying his face for a length of time was when you were about six or seven, and he appeared on TV along with the military governor, commissioning a road or bridge that his company had built.

"I did my best."

You smile. "If, God forbid, you have another daughter, BB, and she's the only child of her mother, and her mother dies when she's eleven, in boarding school, and you send her to stay with her mother's only brother and his wife who maltreats her, and you never visit her, and you finally acknowledge her publicly when she's in her twenties because she's too big and too wild to stay hidden anymore, and you never did anything for her except send money—please don't tell her . . ." You pause, exhale. "Please don't tell her that her ginger tea is abominable."

You both chuckle over that, and he almost chokes in relief.

The waiter comes with a teapot of hot water, a fresh teacup and saucer, a balloon glass half-filled with what you know is Courvoisier VS Cognac, BB's poison of choice. As always, whenever they bring BB's drink, you bob your head as you sing the hook in Busta Rhymes's "Pass the Courvoisier," and BB watches you, bemused. Eventually, the drinks are set, and the waiter leaves. You sip your tea, and he gently swirls the brandy but doesn't drink.

"It must have been very hard for you."

For a moment, you consider sharing a fraction of your considerable baggage. Like how your first period came suddenly during business studies class in JS 2, and the other children, innocently cruel, laughed as you leaked red and dashed to the bathroom, but there was no tissue paper, so you had to use your handkerchief and socks to stanch the flow, and you cried at first because you didn't know why you were bleeding, and you thought you were going to die, but later, you didn't mind dying because, maybe, you'd see your mother again. Or like the time you were twelve and you ran away from your uncle's house in D-line and trekked across the railway and the fruit market, across Aba Road at Traffic Light, and up Nzimiro Street into Amadi Flats because all you knew about BB's address was that he lived somewhere in Amadi Flats, and you were determined to knock on every gate in Amadi Flats till you found him. And at the fourth gate, an elderly woman let you into her house, spoke kindly to you, and gave you cold orange juice and shortbread biscuits. And while you ate, the police she'd called came. And you all got in her car, they took you back to your uncle's house, and you would always associate shortbread biscuits with betrayal.

Instead, you sigh and say, "You don't want to know the half of it."

He searches your face for a long moment as some truths, gently like earth-sipping dew, dawn on him. Eventually, he whispers, "I understand why you hate me."

You smile. "I don't hate you anymore, BB. You no longer have that power over me. God has fixed me."

Oritsejolomi.

Two years ago, you'd just been discharged from the clinic in Abuja. You'd stepped out from the private room where you'd spent three days, into the corridor, on your way out, a nurse by your side, when he said, "I never thought we'd meet like this."

You turned and there he was, in a wheelchair, vaguely familiar.

"I saw you at Femi's housewarming party," he explained. He rolled up to you. "I'm Jolomi."

It came to you. "Ah, yes. I remember you." Three weeks before. Striking man, magic smile, rough-curled hair, fashionable stubble; and it seemed like both of you caught yourselves stealing glances at each other. Now, he was broken, held together by casts on his right leg and left arm, a neck brace, and a bandaged crown.

"I'm Ukela," you say.

"I know. You designed Femi's house. And Alhaji Tukur's office. I like how you maximise small spaces." He winced slightly as he talked.

"Thank you. What are you doing here?"

"I get tired of staying in my room, so I take short rides with this." He patted the motorised wheelchair. "Looks like I'm next door to you."

"I've just been discharged. I meant, what happened to you?"

He glanced away. "Accident. My car flipped four times. Thankfully, nobody else was hurt." He regarded you. "I see you've been in an accident or lost someone in one?"

"Lost someone. My mother. How did you guess?"

"Something about your face when I mentioned the accident. And I sense things. I'm sorry about your mother."

You chanted your rote response. "It's okay. It happened a long time ago."

His eyes told you he didn't believe you. "What brought you here?"

You smiled but didn't answer the question. "Take care. I guess I'll see you around sometime," you said as you left.

You saw him the next day when you returned for a follow-up injection. After you were done, on impulse, you asked the nurses if you could see him. You found him in the room on the bed. His grin, when he saw you, was as big as life and made you smile. "I knew I'd see you soon," he said.

"Yeah? Why's that?"

His eyes twinkled. "I told you yesterday. I sense things."

You wondered how he read you easily. "Yeah right. I was in the building. Thought I should pop in and say hi."

"Okay. Keep me company for a while. Please. Come sit."

You went. You sat. You talked. And that was how the unspoken routine of daily visits started. It was easy because the clinic was just down the street from your house in Wuse. Conversations grew longer every day fueled by ice cream from Cold Stone, which you snuck in for him (he had an addiction). Because he read you easily, silences were easy, excellent; and talking became part conspiratorial, part confessional for both of you. A week after you met, he admitted that he was an alcoholic and he'd been driving drunk when the accident happened. It was his second drunk-driving accident in eighteen months, and he feared he would not survive a third. That was when you told him about your seizure from the Tramadol overdose, which had admitted you in the clinic. You also told him about the times you cut yourself as a teen. He asked if your overdose was deliberate. You said you didn't know. After a long silence he said, "We have to choose if we want to live or die. Whatever we choose, let's do it. Do it with our chests." You wondered if he was joking.

You watched them remove his neck brace, and he twisted his head and beamed. You were there when he was discharged and sent home, still with the casts on. You helped him remove all the alcohol in his house. You took him through a taste test for substitutes until he finally chose energy drinks, and you discovered ginger tea. To lessen the odds of him getting drunk and getting behind the wheel, you got him to employ a driver. You watched him force himself to stand again, to walk small steps with crutches. You were there when they took the bandage off his head, leaving three heavy scars on his scalp, which meant a barber had to shave him bald. The loss of his hair distressed you, and it didn't help that he joked about it, calling himself Gorimapa. Eventually, he explained, "Laugh or cry, I can never grow a full head of hair. I might as well laugh."

You told him about BB and your mother. You told him about the time when you were seven, when some boys had shot at a tiny bird with their slingshots. The bird had swooped to eat something on the ground when they hit it. It tried to fly off with one broken wing, but it careened and crashed, disoriented, by the front door of your mother's flat. You opened the door quickly, snatched the bird, and shut the door in the faces of the onrushing boys. From outside, they asked you to return their bird, and when you refused, they threatened to beat you when next they saw you. You didn't go outside for three days while you determinedly nursed the bird, trying to force-feed it breadcrumbs and rice. You told him he reminded you of the bird. He asked what happened to the bird. You replied that it died. Joking, he begged you to stop nursing him.

Your relationship grew to this nebulous thing. He intrigued you. You knew he was attracted to you, but it was frustrating that he never said or did anything about it. You still went on dates with other people, spent nights and weekends with them, and Jolomi knew, but you always returned to him like he was home. You spent a lot of time together; you'd even napped with him on his bed, cuddling him. He instructed his chef to cook meals for you daily, and his driver delivered them to you at work or at home if you weren't in his house.

One night, you lost it.

It didn't help that you were slightly drunk and had just returned from a terrible blind date where the man kept trying to run his hand up your thighs under the table. You got to Jolomi's house and found him in his bathroom, leaning on one crutch in front of the mirror and using his free hand to sponge-bathe himself. You hugged him from behind. He smiled at you from the mirror. You took the wet sponge from him. You'd sponge-bathed him a few times before. You knew what to do. Still standing behind him, you cleaned him till you reached between his legs, and his semi went hard, as always. Usually at this point, you'd smile at each other, saying nothing. You'd finish the bath and help him dress. That day, you stroked him instead, running your thumb across the tip, watching him in the mirror as he groaned.

"Stop." He held your hand.

"What?"

"Stop. Please." His voice was stronger.

"What the fuck, Jolomi? You think you're too good for me."

"I never thought or said that."

"Then what is this nonsense? Everybody else would like what I was doing."

"I like what you were doing. But I'm not everybody else."

"Well, excuse me, Mr. High and Mighty. For the record, you're not all that. And you've got a small dick."

He snorted. "But you were all over it a minute ago."

"So, you're judging me now?"

"For that? No. But for stupid shit like sleeping with people to get briefs when you don't need to? Hell yes, I'm judging you for that."

"I knew it. I knew you always thought you're too good for me because you know my body count. You're just like other men."

"Don't be silly."

"Fuck you, Jolomi. You don't own me. I can fuck anyone I want, and I refuse to be slut shamed for it."

"Yeah? Try to remember this the next time you complain that casual sex is ultimately unfulfilling. Or the next time you cry yourself to sleep about it. Don't worry—I won't say, 'I told you so.'"

You shook your head. "You think you're better than me?"

"I think you're better than this shit. You're a smart woman, a brilliant architect, but right now, the first thing, the main thing you know how to offer is sex. And when you meet a man who wants more than sex, who sees through all your shit and still likes you, you can't process it. Maybe it's because you really don't like yourself. Maybe that's why you always self-sabotage. Like you did with Victor." He read the look on your face. "Wait. You thought I didn't know about Victor and why you relocated from Port Harcourt to Abuja?"

"You don't know me." This comes out as a whisper.

"I know enough. Right now, you're a cartoon, a stereotype. You're every girl with daddy issues. Fucked-up childhood? Check. Absent or uninterested father whom you love-hate but can't stop vying for his attention? Check. Party girl and sex freak in public? Check. Manipulative, depressed, self-harming, self-loathing mess in private? Checkity-check. What else have I missed? Oh yeah. You rock the biggest pity-parties, always feeling sorry for yourself, always the victim. Life has been cruel to you. Yes. But your head is stuck so deep in your own arse you don't realise you've been blessed too. Burdens and blessings. Just like everybody else."

He sighed, and his voice went soft. "You're nobody's victim,

Ukela. I don't know how you're going to do it—God or therapy—but you need to unfuck your mind big time. Save yourself."

"Oh yeah? Okay, Mr. Physician, who can't heal himself. Remember to save yourself the next time you relapse with your drinking. Don't worry—I won't say, 'I told you so.'"

You want to break down, tell him that of all the men who'd hurt you, he'd just cut you the deepest, but you steel yourself and lash out instead. "You know what? Goodbye, Jolomi. I hope you relapse. I hope you drive yourself when you're drunk and you crash and die."

"I'm . . ." BB hesitates before it comes out. "I'm sorry."

For a man like him, apologising for anything is a big deal, but you shrug like it's no big deal. And you search your soul, and at this moment, it isn't. Or maybe you're numb and don't care anymore. Whatever it is, you don't feel the familiar pain, and you're thankful.

"As a man gets old, he realises some of his mistakes. Some he can make right, some he can't." He sighs. "Tell you what—when we finish our drinks, let's go to the house together. It's time for you to finally meet some people."

You are thirty-three years old, and you've never been in your father's house or met his wife and your half brothers. No, viewing Facebook profiles didn't count. You sigh. "I'm not sure I want to meet your family." You shrug. "I'm sorry. I don't know what to call them."

"They're your family too."

You roll your eyes. "If you say so, BB." Then you say, "This is a surprise. I'm not sure I'm mentally ready to do this. Especially today. Or ever."

He sips his cognac. "Don't worry. They all know about you. Besides, you're not meeting any of the boys today. They don't live with me anymore. Just my wife."

"I'll think about it."

He regards you again. "You look different. Content."

You nod. "I am content. For the first time in my life. I'm still learning how to enjoy it. Anyway . . ." You smile. "I came down here and called this meeting because there's someone I want you to meet."

BB raises an eyebrow with a half smile on his face. "I see. I hope you chose well this time." It's the gentlest of rebukes about Victor.

"I used to be the queen of terrible choices, but for this one, I think I got it right."

"He can take care of you?"

You go all Destiny's Child. "I make my own money, BB, and . . ." The frown on his face stops you. You exhale. "Yes, BB, he can take care of me. He already does."

"And he loves you more than you care for him? This is important because us men, many times we—"

"Ahn-ahn, you've been my father for only two minutes, and you're already overdoing it. I swear, I already miss the way we were."

He wrinkles his nose. "When you finish, please answer my question."

You chuckle. "I suspect so, but how do you measure these kinds of things?"

"You'll know." Sip. "So, where is he?"

"Oh, there." You point to the bald man sitting alone at a table in a corner of the restaurant, watching both of you while nursing a Red Bull. You signal for him to come over, and he flashes his magic smile as he walks to your table.

You do the introductions. "This is my father. You can call him BB. Dad, this is Oritsejolomi. Call him Jolomi."

"In the City"*

Tuesday, 7:13 p.m.

Corporal Enenche had hoped he wouldn't kill anybody today.

But the boy running away from him was testing that resolve. He was blur fast, sprinting hard through the narrow, labyrinthine alleys of the shanty town that was Asiama Waterside.

Enenche was an athlete—weekend runs, fourth in the four hundred metres, and third in the eight hundred metres at the last Police Games—but he hadn't planned on exerting himself this evening. Plus, he had felt his trousers rip again (he had patched them twice before) as he started chasing the boy; and his old shoes, stretched at the sinews and straining not to tear apart, screamed as they took the punishment of him pounding the earth.

Running with his rifle in his left hand was ungainly, but Enenche was confident that he would catch the boy. Asiama Waterside was a maze, but he knew it well, having lived there until six weeks ago, and it was unlikely the boy would give him the slip. The boy's speed,

* Written under the influence of "In the City" by Brymo

adrenaline-fuelled, could only carry him for a short distance. He would tire the longer the chase went on, and Enenche, full of stamina and cold-burned rage, would be on him. The beating promised to be thorough and within an inch of the boy's life—payment for his trousers and his shoes (if they survived the run).

But he would not kill the boy as he may have casually done in the past.

Lately, Enenche had been going through an existential crisis (though he didn't know what it was). He'd also been afflicted with a vicious insomnia that allowed him three hours of nightmare-cursed sleep, on average, at night. Then, on a bus one day along Creek Road, he'd met Tariebi, a widow with a gentle, ready smile that belied her steel underneath. He'd tried to chat her up, but she collared him by preaching about Jesus and repentance. He laughed at her, but they got talking and got off at the same stop at Asiama Waterside (he was still living there then), where she handed him a tract. On impulse, he'd half jokingly asked her to pray for him and was pleasantly surprised that she did—there by the side of the street, eyes open and smiling, voice low and steady like they were conversating. That night, he slept, still for three hours but, for the first time since he killed his first man, without nightmares. Two days later, he got a letter—he'd applied and interviewed for the role of a supervisor in a security company that provided guards for the residences and offices of the wealthy, a job with better pay and less risk than the police. They'd offered him the job, to start in three months, and he put in his notice to the police and began counting down.

Enenche was a superstitious man. Convinced that Tariebi had turned his luck, he took to courting her at her salon, a shack in Asiama Waterside, with the long-term plan of marrying her to hold her good luck at his will, like a genie in a lamp. Though his nightmares came back, his belief in her was unshaken. She continued to herd him off by threading Jesus in their conversations. He listened, not because she was converting him, but because he liked her voice—it was husky like she had a dying cough stuck in her throat and drawled like she was stoned mellow, and it soothed him. He joked that he'd happily take a day-long nagging from it. With her and with the new job coming, his demons grew calmer, and his bloodlust began to numb. Then today, he decided that he wasn't going to kill anyone till he left the police in three weeks.

But this running boy was tempting him. They ran silently through paths and people. Enenche matched him, duck for duck, weave for weave, leap for leap, ensuring that he was always in sight. The boy was wearing a black T-shirt and jeans, and in the falling light of dusk with part of the sky already blackened, the coming night would camouflage the boy if they ran for a few minutes more. However, he was also wearing white sneakers, helpful like glow lamps to Enenche. He decided it was time to end the chase. He stretched his legs, turbo-bursting suddenly, but the boy seemed to sense this. He vaulted a puddle, and in one smooth motion, used his landing as a spring to turn right, sharply, into an alley. Five seconds behind, Enenche leapt over the puddle, but as he landed, his left shoe sighed and half tore, vamp and toe cap, from the sole. He pulled up short and raised his leg to study the shoe to fully appreciate the betrayal. As he planted his foot back on the muddy ground, the wetness poured in through the open mouth of his now-laughing shoe, seeped through his sock, and licked his toes. He made a quick decision, but it cost him valuable time—he paused and tore off both shoes, as running with them would slow him. His socks would also be ruined by the end of the night, and they were his favourite pair. His anger, even-keeled and controlled till then, tipped over, scorching reason.

That was when, subconsciously, he decided he was going to at least shoot the boy.

Tuesday, 11:48 a.m.

Godson was nervous.

He was supposed to meet the woman by noon at her salon, but he was already there. He didn't know whether he should wait outside till it was time or go in now. He didn't want to seem desperate.

He was desperate.

He needed this job. His mother was just recovering from tuberculosis and he, her only child, had been her sole caregiver. Paying for antibiotics, doctor visits, masks he had to wear to protect himself, antiseptics, and cleaning agents had swallowed his meagre savings. They managed to get by because his mother's boss kindly allowed him to fill in for her, in her job as a street sweeper, during the months she was quarantined at home. With his mother back on her feet and about to resume work on Monday, it was time for him to find his own job.

He hadn't done this type of work in seven months. For the millionth time, he hoped the fact that he was a man wouldn't prevent him from getting this job. Usually it didn't, but one never knew—some owners simply didn't want men.

He pulled the collar of his shirt and gently dusted soot off his shoulder. He had taken care with how he looked that morning: lightly starched white shirt tucked neatly into dark-blue jeans over black loafers. He'd worried about wearing the white shirt because lately, soot from the many illegal and crude oil refineries called kpo-fires had blanketed the air in Port Harcourt and settled on everything like a plague of black motes. But finally, he wore it because it was his best shirt, and he wanted to make a good impression. His mother had approved the look before he left. She'd prayed for him too.

Now, apart from the ubiquitous black soot, he also hoped the look would keep fresh till he went into the salon. The sun burned smack in the middle of the sky, stunting shadows to a useless shortness so they were unable to provide shade. It was sweltering, the heat thicky-thick, and the sweat poured from him so much that he was concerned about sweat rings. This made up his mind for him—he would go in now. He wiped his face carefully with a clean handkerchief. He took a deep breath, held it for a long moment, and exhaled.

Then he walked to the salon.

Tuesday, 7:17 p.m.

Enenche turned into the alley, but the boy had disappeared.

He cursed the boy and the boy's father and genealogy, wherever they may be. But his mood improved quickly when he realised there were no outlets from the alley—it led straight down to the Dockyard Creek, which ran behind the Old Township area of Port Harcourt. He would have to do a door-to-door search on all the shack houses in the deserted alley. He considered calling Sergeant Shehu and the others in his patrol team to cordon off the area while he searched, but he remembered that he couldn't tell them exactly where he was because the alleys and streets of Asiama Waterside had no names. He cursed them, the lazy cowards, for falling back at the start of the chase and letting him go after the boy alone.

He decided to start with the first shack on his left. It was made with rusted corrugated iron and wood set in an uneven cement base, which made it tilt slightly. The door was old plywood—solid as a biscuit.

He took a shooting stance—steadied the rifle butt in the pocket of his right shoulder, cheek on the cold stock, holding the pistol grip with a finger by the side of the trigger guard. He approached the shack.

He raised his left hand and knocked on the door.

Tuesday, 11:57 a.m.

The woman seemed surprised when Godson gave her his CV and a photocopy of his SSCE certificate.

She smiled, glanced at the papers, and told him she'd read them later. First, she wanted a practical test of what he could do. He told her he had pictures of his past work. She asked to see them. He opened his phone, carefully searched for the correct folder, opened it, turned the screen to her, and slowly flipped.

She sat opposite him, reclining in one of the leather salon chairs with a washer attached to it, and the distance between them meant she couldn't see his screen clearly. Reflexively, she signalled for him to hand her the phone. He hesitated so long that when he finally offered it, she smiled and shook her head. She told him to stand beside her and show the pictures himself. He felt embarrassed that his fear of anyone going through his phone was so obvious.

The pictures were of the faces and heads of different women, taken to highlight the hairstyles he had made. There were weaves, braids, perms, and natural styles. She studied each picture carefully, asking questions. When he finished flipping through the pictures, she asked if there were any videos of him doing any of the styles so she could be sure he was the one who'd done them. He hesitated again. There were videos, but they were in a folder with other videos he didn't want her, or anyone, to see. So, he lied and said he had no videos. Then he added that he could give her the numbers of five of his customers who could vouch for him.

She asked what his strengths were. He said he was great with cutting and styling weaves, fixing closures, making wigs, and braids. He added that he was average with natural hair and mani-pedis. She seemed satisfied with this and began to read his CV. He glanced around. The salon was small and neat, walled with new plywood, painted white. It was furnished with the usual paraphernalia of hair dryers, washers, and salon chairs. The Formica-covered shelves and worksurfaces were stacked with hair extensions and products. A medium-sized generator rattled outside.

She looked up from her reading and asked if he was really twenty because he looked sixteen.

He heard this regularly. He confirmed that he was twenty.

She observed that he did well in SSCE and asked if he had any plans for university.

He replied that he had none for now; his focus was on working so he could take care of his mother.

She asked about his father.

Godson, who had never known his father because the man

had walked out one day when he was a baby and never came back, gave his standard response that his father died just after he was born.

Tariebi regarded him for a long moment. A widow herself, she considered it a duty to help another widow by employing her son, especially as he was a star-quality hairdresser. Plus, there was something about the boy. He lived in Asiama Waterside, arguably the place with the most crime, drugs, and disease in Port Harcourt, but he carried himself like he was a pilgrim, passing through to another place where he truly belonged, and nothing appeared to have stained the white of his spirit. Inexplicably, she felt drawn to protect him.

She asked if he could start work tomorrow.

His smile was a perfect thing—even white teeth and dimples deep enough to bury a diamond. And for the first time, she noticed what a beautiful boy he was.

Tuesday, 7:22 p.m.

There was no answer to Enenche's knocking.

He paused and listened. No sound came from inside the shack. There were no lights either. Enenche raised a foot and put his heel through the already-rotting door. It fell open. He took a step but stood at the doorway, half in, half out, so he could keep one eye on the alley for the boy. Quick scan of the room. Flimsy mattress, strewn clothes, dirty pots, a bucket. But nobody.

He backed out.

On the alley, he made for the opposite shack. Then, the wind changed direction, and suddenly, he caught the savoury aroma of stew someone was cooking. For a moment, it overpowered the usual briny, urine-y, sewer-y smell of Asiama Waterside. It was so heady that he stopped and inhaled, greedily drinking every drop of the smell.

It dulled his edge at once. It reminded him that he was hungry, and he hadn't eaten since morning when he had yam and beans without meat at his favourite Mama Put. It also made him unexpectedly reconsider his priorities. Enenche remembered that he was leaving the police in three weeks. He should be taking things easy. He shouldn't be the one chasing the boy, a petty drug peddler, through the dangerous alleys of Asiama Waterside while Sergeant Shehu and the others chose the easy task of confiscating the boy's stash. Enenche was a superstitious man. He considered that he had torn his trousers and killed his shoes, and continuing the chase may bring further bad luck. Better to turn back now and make the best of the night. Enenche hoped the boy's stash would be shared later among the team, and there would be something for him to smoke tonight.

It was at that moment that the door of the shack he was facing swung open, and a youth stepped out, paused by the doorway. In that fragment of time, before he closed the door behind him, he was silhouetted by the flickering candlelight from inside the house, and his shadow fell long and wavy into the alley.

Enenche caught a glimpse. He wore dark clothes but something shifted Enenche's mind through several gears.

He wore white sneakers.

Enenche wasn't sure this was the same boy he'd been chasing. This one appeared casual, at ease, about to go out for the night. But his brain screamed, *White sneakers! White sneakers!*

The boy stiffened his surprise when he saw Enenche.

Enenche barked, "Hol' it! Police!"

Tuesday, 12:09 p.m.

Eminem watched Godson walk out of Graceland Salon and called out to him.

Godson turned, paused his walk, and waited for Eminem, who bounced over, and they fell in step.

They shook hands, clicking fingers, and Godson asked, "Emmy, how far? What's up?"

Eminem bobbed his shoulders. "Steppin' up my hustle, bro. Doing it big time. Big time!"

"Yeah?"

"Yes o. I wan tell you the news, so you know what's up. What's up."

"The news?"

Eminem popped his collar, which was imaginary as he was wearing a T-shirt, black. "Which one you want? Kush, skunk, white, crack—pure or mixed, anyhow you want. Even cocaine sef. You want any one? I supply. Any one. Free delivery sef for Waterside." He chuckled.

They had been classmates at Baptist High School. Though not top of the class like Godson, Emmanuel, or Eminem, had also been a good student. They weren't friends, but there was a mutual respect that came from growing in the same school and neighbourhood and hanging out in similar circles.

Godson paused before he replied, "What about your pharmacy work?" The last he knew, Emmy worked behind the counter at the unlicensed neighbourhood pharmacy selling the usual mix of antimalarials, analgesics, antibiotics, and condoms for the always-scowling pharmacist whom everyone called doctor.

Eminem stopped mid-walk, bent to wipe his white sneakers. He frowned because he only succeeded in leaving black streaks on them. He pulled a white handkerchief, dabbed his face, and looked at it. More black streaks. He muttered, "Kpo-fire. God punish una." He sighed and refocused on Godson. "Pharmacy? Forget the pharmacy. I'm doing my own thing now. I be entrepreneur. Entrepreneur!"

"I hear you, Emmy."

"This pharmacy talk reminds me—I can also get Tramadol and codeine if you want. Good price." He nodded like there was music playing that only he could hear. "Now you know what's up. So, you go buy from me? Remember, I be your guy o. Your guy!"

Godson decided it was best that he pat his pockets and shrug.

"No wahala. Spread the word sha. Tell your friends to tell their friends, so we can be friends. You get me?" He sniggered. "Tell them to ask for Eminem. Eminem!"

"Okay, Emmy."

He slipped on his fake Versace shades. "Eminem, bro. Call me Eminem now."

Tuesday, 7:10 p.m.

Sergeant Shehu observed the boy in the white sneakers.

The boy hung a satchel off one shoulder, and his walk was an exaggerated strut, which irritated Shehu. But the boy didn't walk off anywhere; he swagger-circled round the same spot at the entrance to Asiama Waterside, a junction of several alleys. He wore sunglasses even though it was dusk, and he constantly bobbed his head.

Four of them sat in the unmarked bus with the engine idling. Shehu was in front with Constable Henshaw, the driver. Enenche and Olotu, both corporals, sat in different rows in the back with Enenche nearer the door.

Shehu watched another boy approach White Sneakers. They shook hands and talked for a moment. Then White Sneakers reached into his satchel and brought out something he fisted to hide. At the same time, the boy pulled some naira notes from his back pocket. Both their hands were full when they shook again, making the switch. White Sneakers put the money in his pocket as the boy straightened the spliff, pasted it on his lips, and walked away into an alley.

Shehu pointed at White Sneakers. "That boy—did he pay anybody?" He pronounced pay as fay.

They understood what he meant. Everyone who dealt drugs in Asiama Waterside was meant to pay a fee to Shehu and his team. They squinted and focused on White Sneakers. He was new.

Olotu, who kept the purse, said, "No. Him no pay."

"Sure?"

"Sure, boss."

"Shege!" Shehu grabbed his rifle and opened the door. "Enenche, Olotu, let's go." He was out of the bus before he finished speaking.

White Sneakers was in the middle of another aimless walking circle and so, he didn't notice Shehu stride up to him. He turned when Shehu tapped his shoulder. The first thing Shehu noticed was how the light bounced softly off the big, gold Versace logo on the stems of the boy's sunglasses.

Eminem looked up at the dark, burly man who was almost a head taller and standing unnecessarily close to him. They faced off for a second, and Eminem rolled a shoulder, leaned in, and snarled. "Wetin?"

The man snatched Eminem's satchel.

Eminem, a veteran of several street fights, played it by the book. He pulled his head back and slammed it forward, hard, using his forehead to smash into the man's nose. The man groaned and fell backwards to the ground.

Eminem towered over the prostrate man and was about to retrieve his satchel when from his peripheral vision he saw a figure rushing at him. Street matador, he sidestepped the lunge at the last second and even threw a punch, which didn't connect properly and glanced weakly off the man's shoulder as he passed.

He danced on the balls of his feet, and in what felt like slow motion, he wondered who these men were and why they were attacking him. Then he saw a third man alight from a bus with a rifle, and all the jigsaw pieces fell into place—though they were not in uniform, they were policemen.

He snapped like a released spring and zapped, lightning bolt, down an alley.

One of the policemen pursued him.

Tuesday, 7:22 p.m.

Godson was having a good day.

He had gotten the job with Tariebi. His mother's hospital tests had come in, and finally, she was all clear from TB. To celebrate, he'd used the last of the unripe plantains in the house and some fish to make kekefia for her. Then he called his on-again-off-again to share the news, and they agreed to meet up at a bar in Borokiri at 8:00 p.m.

Godson, fresh from a bath and a dash of perfume, dressed quickly in a navy-blue T-shirt and jeans. He considered wearing the black shoes he'd worn earlier today, but at the last minute, he changed his mind and chose his white secondhand Nikes.

Ready, he knocked on his mother's door and told her not to wait up for him. Their house was just two tiny rooms. His mother stayed in the bedroom, and he slept in what was supposed to be the living room where they received guests. They cooked in the open at the backyard, which also housed a rectangular tube of old zinc sheets about the height of a man that served as a bathroom. The toilet, a plywood shack on stilts over the Dockyard Creek, was down the street, and everyone shat in the river.

Before he left, he called out to his mother again to remind her to put an eye on the burning candle, stuck partly in a bottle.

He opened the door, stepped outside, and closed it behind him.

He waited for a moment for his eyes to adjust to the darkness.

He heard a sound like someone was moving, and he turned his head in the direction where it came from.

It seemed there was a man with a rifle up, pointing at him.

Surely this was a mistake.

He realised it wasn't a mistake when he heard: "Hol' it! Police!"

Tuesday, 7:35 p.m.

"This is not the boy na."

The man who said this was gingerly nursing his nose like it hurt. There were two other men with him, and they sat in a beat-up bus cradling rifles, brooding, foreboding.

The man who arrested Godson said, "I know, sir. Sometime you set trap for elephant, but it catch antelope."

The men laughed like it was some inside joke Godson wasn't part of. They made him, prey in the middle of the wolf pack, sit on the ground while they surrounded him and barked rapid-fire questions.

"Oya, identify yourself. Who are you?"

"Your name is Godson? Godson who?"

"Where's your ID?"

"You mean you don't have ID card?"

"I think he's a militant. You want to be the next Doughboy, abi?"

"No. He have soft face. Are you drug boy or Yahoo boy?"

One of the men leaned over and burrowed through Godson's pockets. "How much you get? Where is your ATM card?" He unearthed Godson's phone, loose change, and keys.

Sore Nose Man asked, "Olotu, how much is there?"

Olotu counted quickly and spat his disappointment. "Four fifty, boss."

Sore Nose Man frowned like there was something bitter in his mouth and declared, "This is not antelope. This na lizard." He shrugged and philosophised, "Anyhow, we must still eat."

Olotu and the other man laughed, but it was hollow, mirthless. The man who arrested Godson didn't laugh but stared dolefully at his gaping shoe, which he had stopped to pick up on the way. Then his face lit up as an idea came to him. He took a step towards Godson and ordered, "Off your shoe." Then, Olotu's sudden slap stung and made Godson's eyes water. It was unnecessary because he was already taking off his Nikes. The man snatched them from his hands and tried one on. It looked big for him, but the man's satisfied smile confirmed that size didn't matter.

Sore Nose Man said, "Let's go. Leave this man. Bad market." Olotu folded the money and put it in the flap pocket of his shirt. They stepped away from him.

Godson began to hope. All he wanted now was to return home and cry in the dark till he fell asleep.

"Wait! Open his phone."

Because they saw that his fear suddenly leapt to terror, because he initially refused to tell them the password for his phone, because he begged them instead for the first time that night, they forced the password from him, but only after breaking two of his teeth and splitting his lip in three places with the butt of a rifle.

It was the man who arrested Godson who held the phone and searched it. Eventually, he got to Godson's videos. They were mostly porn clips, but they were all of a peculiar category. His mouth fell open.

"You are a gay? Hey!"

That was when Godson knew he wasn't going home tonight.

Tuesday, 9:56 p.m.

Enenche had hoped he wouldn't kill anybody today.

They handcuffed the boy to a seat in the back of the bus and resumed their patrol round Old Township. From the front seat, Shehu asked him to name other gay men he knew, but he didn't talk. In a flash, Shehu half turned, swung his rifle, and aimed it at the boy. Calmly, but with cold-burned anger in his voice, he threatened to waste the boy, rationalising that life was already wasted on his kind anyway. Shehu's men knew he was hot-headed enough to start shooting as the bus bounced along the bumpy roads, and they didn't want to catch any stray bullets. Luckily, Enenche noticed and explained why the boy couldn't talk: he was lying on his back, and his mouth was filled with blood, causing him to gurgle and cough repeatedly. They ordered him to turn to his side, he retched up a thick stream of blood, and they temporarily uncuffed him so he could take off his T-shirt to mop the mess. To calm themselves down, they smoked some of the other boy's joints as they drove silently in the night.

The unspoken plan was to take him to the station. Eventually, someone would come to bail him, and as usual, they'd pass a chunk of the bail money to their ogas higher up the food chain and split what was left.

The plan changed when the call came on the radio. An armed robber had just attacked a man on Banham Street. Since they were in the area, they were ordered to pursue. They exchanged knowing glances as the description came in—navy-blue T-shirt and jeans. Without speaking, Olotu went to the back of the bus to double-check. The boy's T-shirt was blood-soaked, but there were still dry patches, which confirmed that it was navy blue. Olotu returned and nodded at Shehu. Shehu whispered to Henshaw.

Enenche knew what was going to happen next.

Henshaw would drive to Cemetery Road and park in the darkness.

Olotu would bring out the boy and handcuff him.

They would lead him through the maze of tombstones to a deserted spot in the cemetery where the grass grew wild and the earth was soft but hungry.

They would ask him to kneel.

Olotu or Shehu would shoot him in the head.

They would remove the handcuffs and carry him back to the bus.

Back at the station, Henshaw would write a report on how they caught and killed the Banham Street robber.

The boy would die, not understanding his death was a grim godsend to this police anti-robbery team—another chance to stat-pad the number of robberies they claimed to have solved.

Before he died though, the boy would understand what was loud but unsaid.

On another day, Enenche too would have shot the boy. But today, he'd decided he wasn't going to kill anybody till he left the police. He had three weeks left.

Inexplicably, he hoped the boy would refuse to kneel when they killed him.

The boy had stopped coughing. Enenche clambered to the back of the bus to him. He lay still, eyes open but expressionless as he regarded Enenche.

Enenche offered him the tail end of a spliff and held it to his broken lips.

They stared at each other for a long moment until, finally, the boy sucked the life out of it in one long, lazy drag.

Wednesday, 12:34 a.m.

Shehu lay naked on his mattress in the dark.

A phone glowed in his hand.

It was the boy's phone. Shehu had removed the SIM card.

A roll of tissue paper was beside his mattress within arm's reach. Next to it were two wads of soiled tissue. Shehu reached for the roll and unfurled some tissue paper.

With his free hand, he opened a video that he had watched five times already.

With his other tissued hand, he reached down to himself.

Wednesday, 12:57 a.m.

As usual, Enenche couldn't sleep.

He was wrapped in his thoughts, waiting patiently till about one a.m. when his three-hour sleep cycle typically started. He hoped he wouldn't dream of the boy this night. After all, he wasn't the one who'd killed him, and God knew there were already enough dead men who tormented him in his dreams.

From his bed, his eyes fell on something placed neatly in the corner of the room. They were his new sneakers, or rather the boy's sneakers.

Enenche considered things for a moment. Then he swung off the bed, picked up the shoes, and put them in his wastebasket.

He lay back in bed. But he wasn't satisfied.

He got up again. He picked up the sneakers from the basket.

He opened the door of his room into the corridor of the Face-Me-I-Face-You where he lived. He placed the sneakers outside his door and shut it behind him. He didn't mind if they were stolen by morning. He was never going to wear them.

After all, Enenche was a superstitious man.

"I Put a Spell on You"*

Buddha said, "My thing has stopped working."

They didn't hear him at first. He had spoken with the softness of a reluctant confessor. They sat round Alex's four-seater dining table, drinking wine and playing straight poker. They played with small bets, a hundred-naira limit per bet, but it was still intense. Buddha had spoken at the end of a round, which Tonse had won, as usual. Tonse's previous winnings were stacked in front of him in neat piles of notes—hundreds, two hundreds, five hundreds, one thousands. As he scooped the latest pot from the centre, he sensed Buddha's listlessness and asked, "How far?"

That was when Buddha sighed and repeated himself. "Guys, nsogbu di. My thing has stopped working." Again, his voice was no more than a whisper, and they had to lean in, strain even, to hear him.

It was Alex's turn to deal. Focused on thoroughly shuffling the cards, he asked, absentmindedly, "What thing?"

---

* Written under the influence of "I Put a Spell on You" cover by Nina Simone

"My praka."

"What is praka?"

Tonse rolled his eyes before he explained. "His particulars."

"Car particulars?"

Tonse clarified again. "He means his equipment."

Alex was still slow to catch on. Maybe it was because he was concentrating more on the cards, or maybe it was because Buddha ran his family's oil tools company (with lots of equipment). He asked, "Which equipment?"

Buddha sighed. "Just negodu this one—forming like he doesn't know the meaning of equipment."

"Ebuka, I don't know the meaning of equipment. Sue me."

Anytime Alex wanted to irritate Buddha, and it was most times, he called him Ebuka, his given name. It wasn't the name—it was his tone and the unspoken conflict between them. It had started nine years ago when Alex had returned from the UK, armed with a master's and a new accent, and declared that he was going to stop calling him Buddha because according to him, it was offensive to Buddhists. (Ironically, it was Alex who had given him the nickname in their early teens.) Ebuka, believing Alex was being a poseur as usual, had replied that he too had lived in the UK for a total of four years (studying for his graduate and MBA degrees), and no Buddhists had complained to him about the nickname. Besides, Alex, who had also just declared himself atheist, shouldn't take Panadol for a headache, which Buddhists didn't have. Alex had smiled, smugly, and insisted on using Ebuka. (However, there would be occasional slips—both in the consistency of his accent and the use of Buddha.) And that was when Buddha, who was raised ajebuttered on all sides, developed his shtick of speaking to Alex with a heavy Igbo accent and mixing English with Igbo.

Buddha said, "Equipment is prick. Penis. Amu. You want me to spell that for you?" Then as an afterthought, he sighed and added, "Ewu! Idiot!"

Tonse's feet drummed a staccato as he snickered. When he was done, he asked, "What do you mean by your praka has stopped working?"

Buddha shrugged. "It just stopped. It no longer receives signals."

"What? How?"

Buddha sighed and slunk in his chair. "I don't know."

"Have you . . . you know . . . tried?"

"Of course, I've tried. I've tried with all my girls." His slow-rolling thunder of a voice dropped to a pitiful rumble. "Nwokem, I need you to look at it."

Tonse's eyes widened. "You mean me?"

"Yes na! You're the doctor."

Tonse raised a warning finger and spoke slowly. "You know I'm an O and G guy, right? I look at vaginas, not penises."

"C'mon . . . just . . . take a look. You may . . . you know . . . observe something. Or you can refer me to somebody. . . ."

"Okay. No wahala."

"Is it possible today?"

Tonse raised an eyebrow. "You mean now?"

"I don't mind."

Tonse shrugged.

"Whoa! No! No! No!" Alex slapped the air, jumped from his seat, and faced Buddha. "What is wrong with you, man? You can't just lay out your penis on my dining table. I eat here, you know?"

Buddha protested his innocence. "I wasn't going to do it here. We'd have gone to the—"

Alex didn't let him finish. "The answer is still no. Nobody is looking at any penises in my house."

Tonse raised a hand. "Alex, you're still vexing that he called you a goat? That small thing? Abeg chill." To Buddha, he asked, "So do you have any problems peeing with it?"

"No, that's fine. It's just that I can't get it to perform anymore . . . with any of my girls."

Tonse asked, "And Moji?" Moji was Buddha's wife.

There was a long pause before Buddha said, uncomfortably, "It works with Moji."

"Then your thing is working na!"

"Not really. It only works with Moji, no one else. I think Moji has jazzed me."

Tonse shot up. "Back up."

"Jazz?" Alex asked.

"Why do you think Moji jazzed you?"

Buddha sighed. "It's a long story."

"Make it short."

Buddha tilted his head sharply as he drained the wine in his glass. As he put down the glass, he frowned and shot an accusing look at Alex. His voice dropped low again, indistinct and hesitant. "Okay. Remember that I made a business trip to Abuja last weekend?"

"Yep."

"There's this girl I was supposed to arrange on that trip. If you see her ehn—fine girl, achalugo nwanyi. It was supposed to be our first jammings. The plan was that she'd spend that weekend with me—"

His phone rang, shutting off the story. He looked at the caller ID and whispered his fear. "It's Moji!"

"We were not talking about you, Moji . . . I swear on my mother's grave." Buddha paced the room as he talked.

Tonse and Alex sniggered.

". . . Okay. Okay. Okay. Leave this matter first. It's a good thing you called sef. Soibi's there with you, right? . . . No, I'm not trying to change the topic. I really want to speak to Soibi. . . . What do I want to talk to her about? Well, we're drinking in her house and we're hungry, and Alex, her silly boyfriend, is too lazy to get us something to eat."

Alex raised a middle finger at Buddha.

"Ah, Soibi. Nwunye anyi, our wife . . . How now? . . . Oh, you heard me? Good. Good. So, I don't have to repeat myself. We're hungry here, but Alex says he doesn't know where anything is in the kitchen. You have spoilt that boy, you know?" He shook his head. "There's fresh fish-pepper soup in the big pot?"

Tonse whooped. Buddha raised a fist as he hailed Soibi. "Ah, Omalicha nwa. Akwa nwa. Chukwu gozie gi."

When Buddha ended the call, he turned to Alex. "And we asked you o. We asked several times if there was anything to eat. Anything to go with this your rubbish red wine." He winced his pain.

"Knowing Alex, he probably thought it's an abomination to eat fish with red wine," Tonse said drily.

"Actually, you're right. Fish and red wine is a faux pas." Alex sneered at Buddha. "But I'm not surprised that you didn't know this, Ebuka. After all, you just called a classic Bordeaux rubbish."

"I don't care what you call it—it tastes like cough medicine and piss." Buddha put his glass on the table. "Abeg, I no dey drink again."

Tonse added, "Shey there's Coke in this house?"

Alex, on his way to the kitchen, pointed to the fridge in the dining room.

"Thanks." Tonse opened the fridge, grabbed a can of Coke, opened it, took a long gulp, and sighed his pleasure. "Ah . . . I needed that to cleanse your expensive plonk off my taste buds. Besides, Coke doesn't act like it's too classy to go well with fish."

"Your father, Tonse! You hear me? I say, your real father!"

Tonse laughed as he shrugged off the yab.

Twenty minutes later, after polishing off two big bowls of fresh fish-pepper soup, Buddha belched, sighed his pleasure, and wiped his lips with a napkin. He studied Alex for a while and sighed again before asking quietly, "Why haven't you married the girl?"

Tonse chuckled and almost choked on his pepper soup.

Alex scowled. "Why do you keep calling her 'our wife'?"

Buddha sighed. "Nwannem, you have not answered my question. You've dated Soibi for long, too long sef. You live together. Apart from us and your mother, she's the only other person who can put up with your crase. You're in love with her. She's crazy about you. So why haven't you done the proper thing?"

As Alex opened his mouth to speak, Buddha said, "And no, don't give me your usual oyibo rubbish about marriage being a dogmatic, sexist, and oppressive sociocultural convention."

Alex smiled. "Okay. What if I told you that Soibi and I agreed not to get married?"

"When was this agreed?"

"When we first met and started dating. That was during our masters."

Buddha rolled his eyes and groaned. "That was nine or ten years ago in London. Dem no send marriage for London. Besides, you were her rebound from that guy she was engaged to but later discovered was already married with kids. What did you expect her to say then? Things have changed now. She . . . could be under intense pressure from her family and . . ." There was something about the way Buddha trailed off that revealed he knew more than he was letting on.

Alex noticed it. He whispered, "Has she been talking to Moji about this?"

"Look, your usual rebellious-to-societal-norms shit may have worked when you were nineteen but, Nwannem, you're forty-three now. Now, no one is going to think you're being contrarian; they'll just assume you're an efulefu. And stop thinking about yourself for once. This is not about you. This is about the woman you claim you love . . . and the child you guys are about to have."

Alex smiled. "So she told Moji?"

Buddha shrugged.

"Congratulations in advance, man," Tonse said. He picked up his forgotten glass of wine. "I've been waiting for a while to toast you on this."

"You knew too?"

"Guy, I've been an O and G doctor for sixteen years. I should be able to tell when a woman is pregnant even when she's not yet showing, yes?" He raised his glass. "A toast?"

"A toast."

Buddha did the honours. "To Alex's child. If it's a boy, may he not turn out to be an onye nzuzu like his father."

"Ise!" Alex replied. "And if it's a girl?"

"Ah . . ." Buddha said. "May God keep her far away from men like us."

They considered it for only a moment. Then, rather enthusiastically, they chorused, "Amen!"

"So, Buddha, what about you and the girl in Abuja?"

"Oh yes . . . so . . . she came to my hotel suite. Mentally, I'm rubbing my hands and licking my lips because of the kind of sweet thing I was going to chop. She stripped, sharp-sharp. She was my kind of girl—ready for action, no plenty grammar.

"And that was when I first knew that I was in trouble. I can't explain it. I mean, I'm there and I know what I'm looking at. It was surreal. My brain is reminding me of what I'm seeing. Naked woman. Silky chocolate skin—real chocolate o, not Choco Milo. I'm looking at ripe bobby, incredible waist-to-hip ratio, even thigh gap sef. I am seeing all these things, but my praka was doing as if I was looking at a mere table. It refused to pick any signal.

"I worried about it for a moment, but I thought, okay, maybe I'm tired, or maybe I had too much to drink. I expected that things would get better once we got going. And as if she could read my mind, she started to blow me. I relaxed, expecting things to pick up. But, mba nu, nothing. Nna men, that was when I realised clap had turned to dance. I start freaking out. Not shouting or anything like that, just silently going mad in my head.

"But this girl, good girl—it seemed like she took it as a challenge. Which was good for me, abi? She went through her amazing repertoire. She blew ooo. She played piano on my body sef. Nothing. No movement. I even started to pray. I mean, as she was blowing, I was praying. Maka Chukwu! The spirit was willing, but the body was weak.

"Eventually, she started to tire. Me sef, at one stage, I stopped feeling sorry for myself and started feeling sorry for her. I stopped her. I said, Nne, it's enough. You have tried. Don't overdo this thing and give yourself locked jaw . . ."

Buddha paused while they guffawed. He even allowed himself a small smile.

"So, we took a break. Ordered room service. Watched a movie. Gisted a bit. She acted as though nothing remarkable had happened, which in a way was correct. Like I said, she's a good girl. Smart, still in uni, but she can school all three of us, easy. We fell asleep. In the morning, we tried again." He shook his head. "Still no action."

"I changed my plans and returned to PH that day. I called up Voke, my regular, and headed straight to her house. Ol' boy, the same thing happened. Praka refused to stand. Guys, I won't lie. I went into Voke's bathroom and wept like a child."

Buddha took a sip of wine without noticing it. "I went home. Moji didn't act surprised to see me. In fact, she was smiling, a one kain smile, like she knew what happened to me. She kept on asking how my trip went, still smiling that gloating smile. That was when I began to suspect something."

Alex snorted his disbelief. "Because she was smiling, you think she jazzed you?"

"Nwannem, I know this woman. I've been married to her for twelve years. She is the mother of my three children. If I tell you that she knew what happened to me, hapu the matter—best believe me."

"Abegi. I don't believe Moji will do that."

"You don't know Moji. She threatened to deal with me if she caught me again with any of my chicks. You only see her sweet and loving public persona. She's like that o, but she's also more vindictive than Genghis Khan."

"Have you tried taking something for it? Viagra?" It was Tonse.

"Guy, I tried that and two other kinds of over-the-counter medication. They didn't work. I'm just forty-two, man. I'm not old enough to be taking this kind of medication and it failing me."

Tonse said, "No be by age."

"So how are you going to treat your erectile dysfunction?" Alex asked.

"Haven't you been listening? It's not erectile dysfunction. I can get it up, but only with Moji."

"Oh, the same Moji who put a spell on your penis. Right."

"Ever heard of magun?"

"Oh, please!"

Tonse smiled. "True story. Guy in my neighbourhood slept with another guy's wife. Died on the spot, the spot being on top the unfortunate woman . . . in her bedroom. Word on the street is that the woman's husband was a renowned connoisseur of jazz." He sighed. "I don't understand people sometimes. They still brought the corpse to the hospital. I don't know if they were expecting a miracle; like I was supposed to play Jesus and raise him up."

Alex said, "Maybe he had a heart attack or something. Where's the autopsy report?"

Tonse laughed. "Abegi. I work with vaginas. I don't do autopsies. Besides—"

Buddha cut in. "Guys, you know my elder brother, Obinna, the pastor . . ."

"Yeah, yeah."

"He screwed this married woman once—"

"As a pastor? Na wa o!"

"No, no, no. This was years ago. He wasn't a pastor then."

"Oh okay. I for don fear. Back to the story."

"So, Obinna shagged this married woman. When he finished, he couldn't pull out."

"What do you mean he couldn't pull out?"

"He just couldn't. He said it was clamped."

"Clamped?"

"Didn't he wait for his praka to fall before pulling out?"

"Praka fell tay-tay. Shrunk to the size of tiny ube sef. He still couldn't get it out. Nna men, the thing ah ji lock down. Maximum security."

Alex threw his hands in the air. "Oh c'mon, guys. Google penis captivus."

"Oh yes. Go on. Please lecture the gynaecologist about penis captivus."

"Tonse, if you want to be treated like a doctor, then talk like one."

"How?"

"You can't be encouraging Ebuka with all his *Africa Magic Yoruba* shit. There is a scientific explanation for everything."

Tonse shook his head. "Alexander Nosakhare Osagie, sorry to burst your bubble, but there isn't a scientific explanation for everything. You, a Bini man, are asking for a scientific explanation for jazz, abi? Continue. Your ancestors would spin in their graves if they could see how much of an educated idiot you've become."

Buddha asked, "What is penis captivus?

"Google it!"

"So how did Obinna resolve the problem of the . . . clamped penis?"

Buddha smiled. "Now, that's the interesting part. He said the woman recited some incantations. And miraculously, he was free."

Alex insisted, "I call bullshit." But there was a hint of a growing doubt in his voice.

Buddha shrugged. "The thing scared Obinna. He stopped chasing women, got serious with God. Hasn't looked back since."

"Buddha . . ."

"Yes?"

Tonse smiled as he said, "It seems people are always trying to damage the penises in your family."

Buddha roared his laughter.

Tonse continued, "You know, you're my man and all. But if your suspicion is true, I can't honestly say I blame Moji. Your waka waka was too much. In fact, the more I think about it, the more I'm forced to have some grudging respect for your wife. She's finally checkmated you." Alex nodded and chuckled.

Buddha shook his head, carefully, like it was heavy and belonged to someone else. "Ah . . . now I know the meaning of the saying 'na who dem catch, na im be thief.' You're laughing today. But you forget that Moji is close friends with your wife and with Soibi too. I pray that Moji shows them the way, and they checkmate you too. Let us see if you will be laughing and having grudging respect then."

The silence fell suddenly, heavy, and uneasy. They wrestled with the weight of unspoken thoughts.

"So, are you going to ask Moji to, erm, free you?" Alex sounded different, concerned.

"Guy, how will I put my mouth to even raise such a conversation?"

"So, what are you going to do?"

"I don't know, man. I don't know."

"Hey . . . wake up."

He had called five times before Soibi stirred. She was a heavy sleeper, preferring long lie-ins on weekends, like today, Saturday.

He was an early riser, partly because he had to leave early for work and mainly because of his insomnia. He sat by the edge of the bed, slipped his hand under the duvet, and gently rubbed the back of her thighs. She slapped his hand, closed her legs, and burrowed deeper under duvet.

He yanked off the duvet, leaving her writhing, naked under the sudden rush of air-conditioned chill. He leered at her body—rangy, a whisper of a baby bump, small breasts with the perkiest nipples in the world (coffee breasts, he called them). But his favourite part of her body was her eyes—big, bright pools of wonder and mischief with lashes so lush that she had never used mascara.

"Oooohh! It's too cold!"

He picked up a mug from the breakfast tray he had earlier set on the table and handed it to her. "Here, coffee." He had made it the usual way—black and unsweetened for himself, creamed and Laser-honeyed for her. (She claimed any other brand of honey would just dull the taste of the beverage.)

She sat up and smiled as she sipped. "Perfect."

He nodded towards the covered plates on the tray and said, "I got you breakfast."

They shared housekeeping and cooking—an agreed rule of their relationship. She made lunches and dinners, and he did breakfasts. It was ironic because he usually didn't eat breakfast, just coffee. She was the breakfast person. "Niiice. What is it?"

"Akara."

It always warmed him, the way her eyes lit up. She loved akara. One of her fondest childhood memories was following her father most mornings to buy akara from a woman who fried them down the street. Then they would eat them, piping hot and greasy, from the newspapers they were wrapped in as her father drove her to school.

"You bought it from Mama Peace? Thanks, baby." When she moved in with him, none of the akara sellers in his neighbourhood would do. Whenever she wanted akara, she insisted that he drive to Mama Peace, her customer in her former neighbourhood, to get some.

"No. I made it."

"You're joking."

"Nope." He placed the breakfast tray over her legs and lifted the covered plates. "Today is your lucky day. You'll finally get to eat the best akara in the world."

He too had some history with akara. His maternal aunt had taught him how to make it when she took him in after his parents died just after his thirteenth birthday. In her shipshape house, akara was twice a week on her meals' timetable: breakfast on Sundays and dinner on Wednesdays. He was responsible for making it and became an expert. So expert that till now, he genuinely believed and boasted that no one made better akara than him. (It didn't matter that the last time he made it was about twenty-five years ago.) Nevertheless, he still hated the process so much that he refused to make it. Till today.

"Awww. Smells nice. Hope it wasn't too stressful to make?"

He shrugged and lied. "It was okay."

She took a tentative bite, hmmed, then gobbled the rest of the akara ball in quick bites. She paused her nippy shoulder dance of joy when she noticed him considering her with an inscrutable smile. Mouth full, she mumbled, "What?"

"Well . . . is it the best you've ever had?"

She nodded and laughed and spat flecks of half-chewed akara. They settled on her chin, chest, coffee breasts, and the bed. He knelt on the bed as he used a napkin to wipe them off her.

And that was when, still on his knees, he said, "Marry me."

"Hello . . . Moji . . . Wait, wait, wait. I have gist. . . . Guess what I'm doing now? . . . Sitting in the bathroom and rocking a beee-yooo-tiful opal and pearl ring on my engagement finger. Alex proposed! Haha! Moji, stop screaming. . . . Yeah, finally. . . . He wants a quick wedding. . . . Within two or three months . . . Mmm mmm, because of the baby and all . . . Yes, I said opal and pearl. You know Alex na. He thinks diamonds are too cliché. . . . Yes, my sister. Thank God o. . . . And thank you, Moji . . . For that thing you gave me na . . . Yeah, I put it in his pepper soup, just like you said. . . . Without it, this wouldn't have happened. Thank you. . . . Hahaha. You can say that again. . . .

". . . Meanwhile, I'll need your help again . . . There is this girl Alex is seeing. She's not even fine sef. . . . She's an intern in his office. . . . He thinks I don't know. . . . WhatsApp na! You know how WhatsApp messages can be hard to delete sometimes. . . . It's not just that he's shagging her—he's friends with her. He tells her almost everything that happens in this house. . . . Are you telling me? I know, my sister. That's how wahala starts. . . . They must break up o. . . . Before the wedding na . . . Abeg, abeg, my day must be perfect. . . . She'll always smell like fowl shit to him? Moji, you're too funny. I love it. . . .

". . . On to more important things, joor. We have a wedding to plan. . . . Venue, décor, cake, photographer, aso ebi. For the white, I'm thinking something angelic, heavenly. . . . All white. I want my wedding pictures to slay. Just like Solange's wedding pictures. . . ."

"I'd Die Without You"*

2013

On the evening of your wife's thirtieth birthday, you sit in the dusk and wonder where you are going to bury your daughter.

You are alone in your car, in the parking lot of the hospital. You've been there for almost two hours, carrying your daughter. Or rather, you've been carrying the shoebox she's curled up in. It's the shoebox for your old Adidas boots, the ones you keep in your car for when you play football on Saturday mornings.

There's another box in the car, on the back seat—the box with your wife's cake. The cake is still there, uncut, rich red velvet, her favourite. The cake, which was from you, was meant to be shared with her colleagues at her office. There are also two cards on the back seat, also from you. She had woken to find them by her bedside that morning. She didn't know about the two more cards you'd planned to surprise her with that day. One card was already on her office desk (the day before, you'd given the card to Sekeghen, her

* Written under the influence of "I'd Die Without You" by P.M. Dawn

colleague, to put it in place before she came in), and the other card was already at Baraka, where you'd planned to take her for dinner after work (the card would have been in the menu given to her). Your plan had been to drop her off at work, wait for her to call you when she saw the card, wait for a second call when they delivered the small chops, wait for another call later in the day when they delivered the bracelet-watch she always wanted, and take her to Baraka after work.

But her water broke that morning. In the middle of rush-hour traffic on Aba Road, worsened by a freak accident involving an overturned trailer sprawled out drunk and cutting the four lanes down to one, you had both sat, squeezed hands, and prayed as the wet mark on her seat spread slowly. To escape the gridlock, you had driven gently on the kerb, oblivious to the curses of pedestrians.

At the hospital, you were calm when they had told you that they couldn't find a heartbeat. And when they said they had to "evacuate" your daughter from her, you'd simply nodded. She'd started crying, softly at first, then in piercing wails that echoed off the hospital's walls and curdled blood. As you held her, told her that it would be okay, that another baby would come, you realised you were bullshitting.

It had taken five years of marriage and two IVFs to get this first pregnancy (despite doctors reiterating that you were both healthy). She had borne all the suffering—the probing and poking by doctors, the numerous injections, and the painful egg aspirations. All you'd had to do was produce sperm samples (and every time, she'd even helped blow you because you had an inexplicable and ridiculous mental block that made it impossible to wank in the fertility clinic).

Back at the hospital, you'd gone numb for the next few hours—

through securing a room, calling her sisters, going back home to pack a bag for her, and the surgery. It was after the surgery, when she was still groggy, being fussed over by her sisters, that one of the doctors tapped you on the shoulder and led you out of the room.

"Sorry to bring this up now. But er . . . we need your decision on how to dispose . . . on what to do with . . . with your daughter. We can take care of her if you prefer, or we can give her to you. . . ."

You took her.

They had brought her out intact. They cleaned her as best as they could before giving her to you. She was twenty-five weeks old. They said she was big, that she looked twenty-nine weeks. She was swaddled in a hospital blanket, ashen, eyes closed, fists clenched, a slight but determined scowl as if death had been a minor irritation she'd overcome. Maybe you were imagining it, but you felt she looked like your wife, which was preferable since you considered yourself an ugly bastard. But you chose to believe she got something from you—hair. She was sprouting soft and curly wisps, which you're pleasantly surprised to see.

Taking her was instinctive, like most decisions you make. You'd had a flash of them dumping her from a truck into an ugly landfill dotted with half-buried arms, legs, and eyeballs from other miscarried babies. You'd realised how silly and ignorant that thought was, but your mind was made. If your wife had been handling things, she would have asked them for specific details of their procedures before making an informed decision on what to do. But you are different, impulsive.

So she ended up in the shoebox, in the car, with you. You spent some of that time in silence. You didn't cry. You really wanted to cry, knowing it would bring some temporary relief from the pain. But try as you did, you couldn't. You talked to her about it. You told her it reminded you of the time when you were ten years old, when your father died, and you couldn't cry. You still haven't cried. You also talked to her about random things—about her clothes your wife had ordered from the US and her room that was just painted pink on Saturday. You touched her hair and told her you'd dreamed she'd have your hair, so you could both rock Afros and take selfies. You touched her cold cheeks. You called her name. Adesuwa. You did not pray.

Eventually, you realise you have to bury her. But where? You wanted somewhere close, but not too close. Somewhere you could visit occasionally. Somewhere quiet and intimate. Port Harcourt Cemetery was too run down and too public to be considered. You couldn't bury her in the compound where you lived—you were a tenant in the left top-floor flat in a building of six flats. Would you dig her up when you moved out? Besides, the compound's floor was paved with interlocked stones. The ideal burial spaces were where cars are parked, and it was just too close for your wife.

You pick up your phone. You had thirteen missed calls from your main man, Ekiyor, while you sat in the car. You had put your phone on silent mode and refused to answer. Now you are ready to talk to Ekiyor. He may know what to do.

You call Ekiyor.

1996

Two months after your eighteenth birthday, you, Ekiyor, and Comfort are sitting in the living room of a dingy house hidden somewhere in Woji. It's the doctor's house. The doctor is a portly man who can't seem to keep still—his head bobbles, he tics, scratches, and gnashes gum. He also can't stop smiling. He unnerves and irritates you, and you hesitate before giving him the money for the procedure.

The money is thirty thousand naira. To raise it, you and Ekiyor had saved, stolen (his mum's jewellery, his father's money, your mum's wrappers), and sold personal stuff (your radio and late father's watch). Ekiyor explained that it cost that much because Comfort was four months pregnant, and most doctors were scared to do it at that advanced stage (officially, it was illegal at any stage, and that was why it was common for it to be done outside hospitals, like this doctor's house). This doctor was the only one who was willing to take the risk, but he refused to budge on his price. So, you raised the money.

The doctor smiles as you give him the money. He tells you not to worry.

You worry.

You've been worrying for two months, since you found out that Comfort was pregnant and she wanted to keep it. She didn't understand why you were so upset or why you accused her of trying to ruin your life or why you insisted that she got rid of it. She had expected you to be happy about it because, as she reminded you, you always said you love her. You remember it differently. Yes, you said you love her, but you only said it in the middle of sex, and in your book, that didn't count. Besides, she was just a house-girl—Ekiyor's family's house-girl, definitely not the right person to raise your child. You don't tell her this, but eventually it sinks in.

Looking back, you'd blame yourself for being naïve and stupid. Unlike Ekiyor, you'd had no game. You'd been tongue-tied around girls and a virgin. Comfort, ditzy but curvaceous, was the only girl who showed any interest in you (which was also strange because she'd rebuffed Ekiyor). Ekiyor had gingered you to go make a move and even talked you through the words you were to drop. His system was from the lady-killers' playbook—charm, chop, clean mouth, move on. But you abandoned the system (it just wasn't you) and actually toasted Comfort with your own words in your awkward, bumbling, roundabout way. When you told him, Ekiyor shook his head and advised, "Don't treat an under-g like a girlfriend."

But at first, your burning hormones and Comfort's ripeness were louder than his words. For a month, you drowned in the girl and the wild pleasures she taught you. Using the pretext of visiting Ekiyor every day (you were best friends from childhood, and it was not unusual to stay at his house till late), you'd sneak into Comfort's room in the BQ and wait till she finished her chores for the day.

Then it started to get boring, not because of the sex—after several embarrassing starts, the sex had grown into something porn stars would be envious of—but because of the vacuity of the girl. Then she had started asking for things you couldn't give, like evening strolls or going to Mr. Biggs together. Then she began to say she loved you (before, during, and after sex) and drop subtle hints about a future for both of you. Then you remembered Ekiyor's words.

You would use the resumption of school for second semester as an excuse to stop visiting. You would think you'd escaped, until she sent a message through Ekiyor that she was pregnant. (Luckily for you, Ekiyor's mum, who would have sniffed out the pregnancy immediately after conception, was in the US for her MBA.)

In the doctor's house, Comfort is slouched in a low chair, legs spread apart. Her long, ugly gown, which meant to conceal, rests instead on her paunch, highlighting it. She's crying, softly, and her swollen eyes make her face even puffier. You feel sorry for her, and you try to tell her this with your eyes, but she refuses to look at you. It had taken a lot to convince her to do this. At first, you'd been gruff, and she refused. You'd learned to be a premium bastard—visiting her regularly, coaxing her, telling her you loved her—before she finally agreed. Even then, you had to come along to make sure she didn't change her mind.

You also told her to give the doctor a fake name—Mercy. You'd explained that this was necessary because the procedure was illegal. It was a lie. You were scared that she might die on the operating table, and you didn't want anything traced to you. You and Ekiyor had given fake names too—Paul and Peter. But you could sense that the doctor knew you were all lying. You could also sense that he didn't care.

You watch the doctor as he counts the money. And it hits you that apart from the whir of his fingers, he is deathly still. After counting, he smiles his satisfaction that it is complete and rubs his palms briskly, almost joyfully.

"Okay. Let's start."

2013

That night, you bury Adesuwa in Ekiyor's parents' house in Old GRA.

It's a house that had been a second home to you since you were little. The shoebox was the coffin, and before you close it, you take off your bead bracelet and place it in her tiny fists. You bury her in the garden, just under Ekiyor's mum's calla lilies. You used to help Ekiyor water and weed them when you were younger.

You remember they used to be white, the common ones. Ekiyor's mum must have planted a new, rarer bush blooming yellow and purple. You cut some flowers and place them on the small mound of earth.

On another day, Ekiyor's mum would have given you an earful for cutting her flowers. Today, she stands behind you and dabs her eyes. Ekiyor's father pats your shoulder. He had said a prayer when the shoebox was placed in the hole. You had played along out of respect for him, but you hadn't bowed your head or said amen. You are still trying hard to cry, but you're too screwed up to manage it.

Eventually, you all return to the veranda and sit in the garden chairs. You take your usual seat, which coincidentally faces the calla lilies. You stare at them. Ekiyor's mum asks for the umpteenth time if she should get you something to eat. You shake your head. She follows your gaze and says, "If you want, I can put a slab there. And maybe a tiny tombstone. . . ."

Ekiyor replies, "Slab, Ma. Small one. No tombstone."

He looks at you for confirmation. You nod. He had read your mind perfectly.

"You should be beside your wife." Ekiyor's father says this gently, but it is still a command. He says to Ekiyor, "Take him back to the hospital."

You recline the seat as low as it would go and ride in silence. Ekiyor turns from Herbert Macaulay into Nzimiro and rolls down the slight hill. He slows by the supermarket at the bottom of the hill, but it's past ten p.m., and the supermarket is closed. He sighs, turns right at the T-junction, and heads up another hill into Ogbunabali. He apologises for the detour. "No vex. I wan buy cigar from aboki."

He spies one and finds a space ahead of it to park. He double parks, but that's okay because Ogbunabali Road is the double-parking capital of the world, and it's night anyway. You feel a sudden need for air, so you walk with him to the corner shack where he buys a pack of cigarettes. As you return to the car, you notice the grandiosely named Hollywood Boulevard Barbing Salon is still open. Pushed by another impulse, you walk in. It's a tiny wooden shack decorated with crudely photoshopped pictures of the barber cutting the hair of celebrities, including Obama and Nelly. The barber smiles his welcome and points you to a seat to wait your turn, as there's a customer on the chair. You tell him you prefer to wait outside.

You join Ekiyor, who's leaning on his car and smoking contemplatively. You reach for his cigarette pack, take one out, and light it. If he's surprised, he doesn't act it. You had quit months ago when your wife announced she was pregnant. You watch the wisp escape from the corner of your mouth. It tastes unfamiliar, even bitter. Maybe it's because it's Benson & Hedges—you were, or are, a Dunhill man. You both watch the sparse traffic go by.

"You think this is God punishing me for . . . that . . . one with Comfort?"

Ekiyor cocks his head. "Oh yeah? So what's He punishing your wife for?" When he said "punishing" he had made the air-quote gesture. He pinches the cigarette from his lips and pokes the air with it. "At least, with you, it was just one—Comfort. With me it was how many sef? Five? Six? So, instead of punishing me, why did He bless me with two kids after I got married?" Then he sighs and punches you playfully on your shoulder. "Don't say ignorant shit just because you're in pain."

The barber pokes out his head and signals that he's ready. As you walk into the barber's shop, Ekiyor whispers, "You really need to learn how to grieve, bro."

And that's how you cut your Afro.

2015

You finally cry on the day your son is born.

But first, you have a row with the doctor who births him.

You and the doctor had a bit of history. You hadn't known he was a doctor then. He showed up one day for weekend football at No. Six Field in Port Harcourt's Old Township. He wasn't one of the regulars like you. You ended up on opposing teams in a five-a-side monkey-posts game, and your team immediately discovered that he was a quick, tricky dancer on the ball. Then he scored that goal. He slalomed past three on your team. You were the last man defending, but he turned you easily, twice, nutmegging you both times, sitting your yansh on the ground the latter time, before rolling the ball for the goal. It was a fantastic goal, and you wouldn't have begrudged him scoring it . . . if not for how he celebrated, or rather how he didn't celebrate. You would have preferred him to smile, laugh, pump a fist, run around screaming. He just popped his collar and did an insouciant half shrug. It reminded you of Cantona's celebration after that goal against Sunderland in '96. And you dislike Manchester United and everyone associated with it.

So, when later, he went on another mazy run, you slide-tackled him, hard.

There are no written rules for weekend football, but there are certain unspoken understandings. Since it was recreational, played by guys with regular jobs and businesses, it was understood that there was no place for hard tackling. Your tackle would have deserved a straight red card in any official match, but there are no referees in weekend football. Luckily for him, he anticipated it and jumped, so the force had ended up only winding him rather than realigning his ankles. You wanted to apologise immediately, but he got up and pushed you, so you pushed back, and a ruckus ensued, and the game ended, and guy-men got in their cars and went home, and there were no usual post-game beers.

And two months later, your wife's contractions start past six p.m., and you take her to the hospital, and she insists on seeing Dr. Tonse, her doctor (the one whom she had repeatedly told you had managed this pregnancy professionally and with great kindness), and you join her in asking for Dr. Tonse, and they call Dr. Tonse, who wasn't meant to be on call that night, and he comes in, and you recognise each other from that day on the football field. And time stops.

You manage to mumble an apology for the tackle, and he arrogantly grunts an indistinct response. Neither of you is satisfied, and the mutual loathing continues. And suddenly, you realise how many times this man has seen your wife vulnerable and even examined her. And you dislike him even more. So, when your wife says she's feeling intense pain in her back during each contraction and wants to start pushing, and he chuckles and says she's not ready, you think he's flippant. And you say so. His riposte is bruising—he ignores you.

Her labour is a brutal fourteen hours. He comes in several times to calm and reassure her; he even makes her laugh. When it's time to take her into the theatre, he lets you in with her but warns you not to be "disruptive." You think he's condescending, but you hold yourself from saying so. Things come to a head when you ask him to give her an epidural (you had seen two seasons of *Grey's Anatomy*, you had Google, and so you knew everything). He ignores you again. You repeat your request. He says no. You tell him you're dissatisfied with his conduct, and you want to make a complaint to his superiors. That's when he calmly tells you to fuck off. It wasn't just a telling off, it was also an order. They eject you from the theatre. Much later, you would learn that he was wary about the epidural because of your wife's low blood pressure, and he had no superiors because he co-owned the hospital.

A few minutes before eight a.m., he walks out of the theatre to the Waiting Room where you and Ekiyor have spent a sleepless night. You both stand up when you see him. His smile is tired but genuine. "Congratulations. . . ."

And that's when you start crying.

You're all surprised by the suddenness and intensity of the tears. Your first thought is that your rep was being damaged because you were crying in front of the doctor. But within a minute, the damage becomes irreparable. Your face is wet, tears and snot flowing in torrents. Ekiyor leads you back to your seat. He and Tonse sit on both sides of you, pat your wracking shoulders occasionally, but don't say anything. Knowing your story, they assume these are tears of joy and relief. They're wrong.

It's your wife who understands why you cry. As you hug her still lying on the bed, she knows you've not even acknowledged your son. She knows you are crying for your late father, for Comfort, for the unnamed one, and for Adesuwa.

"It's going to be okay," she whispers. "It's going to be okay."

"Beautiful War"*

Kenwi

Perhaps you should have lied when your wife asked, "What does she do better than me?"

But you told the truth.

In your defence, you usually told the truth, gall bitter as it may be. That was who you were. It was also the agreed rule in your marriage. The rule was old, from the ten years you and Wobia dated through seven years of marriage.

Even during the three delirious months when you fell feverishly fast for Tamara and happily lost your mind, technically, you didn't break the rule by lying—you just never mentioned her. And when Wobia found out about Tamara, you still didn't lie. And it wasn't because of the messages on your phone, which were borderline incriminating, and which, had you been as honey tongued as Tonse, your elder brother, you would have easily talked your way out of. You simply couldn't lie, convincingly or otherwise.

---

* Written under the influence of "Beautiful War" by Kings of Leon

So, you told the truth then. After Wobia's shock and her tears that flooded for days, after your on-loop grovelling apologies and promises to be a better husband, after your ending it with Tamara (on impulse, on speakerphone, with Wobia present) and deleting her number from your phone, finally, Wobia said she'd forgiven you.

Grateful, you vowed to be more honest, open. You told her that Tamara was the only person you had cheated on her with. You told her all your passwords. She was quieter, withdrawn, but you knew you had to give her time. It took a week before you touched her, but she lay frozen on the bed, and you stopped the kisses and hugged her instead, and she recoiled and stiffened at your touch, and you still held on, and you said you were sorry, and you were really sorry, but she didn't thaw.

You were scheduled to go back to the oil platform on the Atlantic, just offshore Asiama Island where you worked the next day, and you hoped that by the time you returned home in three weeks, things between you and Wobia would have gotten back to normalish.

Then, the morning you were scheduled to leave, Wobia woke you gently. 4:12 a.m.

And she asked you that question.

And you told her the truth.

Wobia

As I sat there listening to Ken talk his nonsense with his oblong head, I began to realise that my whole life with him was a lie.

"Blah-blah-blah . . . she seemed to understand me more . . . blah-blah-blah . . . I was connecting better with her. . . ." Clap for yourself. Mr. Nokia, Connecting People. So, this girl who's known you for a few months is suddenly connecting better than me who's known you almost all your life—from when you were an awkward boy with oversized glasses and ashy knees.

"Yen-yen-yen . . . sex felt different . . . yen-yen-yen . . . blowjobs." Ha! You're talking about sex? I gave you your first kiss, which you slobbered through, remember? Me, Wobia, I disvirgined you, remember? Well, we were both virgins, and it was two days after our wedding, but the point still stands.

I thought all these things, but I didn't tell him. Instead, I went quiet, clenched my jaw, determined that my tears would not fall. They didn't.

He stopped talking. "Are you okay?"

I nodded.

"I'm really sorry. I didn't want to mention it, but because you asked, and . . ."

Now you're blaming me for your turning to a mumu because that girl swallowed every time she gave you a blowjob. It's like she gulped your common sense away, bit by bit. By the way, nobody can convince me that women who swallow actually enjoy it. That thing is like salted vomit that hasn't acidified yet. But I bet she smacked her lips, smiled as she swallowed, and you stupidly believed it tasted like ice cream to her. Ugh. You disgust me, I swear.

But all I said was, "It's time for you to go."

"There's still time. The chopper doesn't leave for the rig till seven."

I shrugged and sidled off the bed.

"You're angry? I'm sorry. I was just trying to tell the truth."

Idiot. You think you can tell "the truth" and just like that, everything would be okay?

I sighed. "I need to go wake Lota and get her ready for school."

"Let me do it. I'll be away for three weeks. I want to bond with her one last time before I go."

I shrugged again. "She's your daughter. Do what you want."

He winced, raised his hand placatingly, and reached to touch my shoulder. I imagined his hand on that girl's shoulder and all over her body. Something about the look on my face made him drop his hand. His sigh was weary.

I walked to the bathroom, turned the tap over the sink, and tried to ignore my trembling hands as I splashed cold water on my face. I kept at it till my hands and resolve steadied. As I went back into the room, he was there with Lota, our five-year-old only child. She, half-awake, nuzzled in his neck, and clung to him like he was the tree of life. Suddenly, I hated how uncanny it was that she looked so much like him—the same frowning nose, wide lips, and sepia skin. The only thing she got from me were her eyes, but they were closed now.

He stroked her hair and whispered, "Say good morning to your mother."

She didn't open her eyes as she mumbled her greeting. On another day, I'd have hugged them both, and we'd all roar, "Monster Hug!" like they did in *Henry Hugglemonster*, and we'd smile and say a quick family prayer. But this was not any other day. So I only kissed the back of her head, careful to avoid touching him.

I stayed in the room while he bathed Lota in our adjoining bathroom, a treat for her as it was bigger and had a tub that she could pretend was a swimming pool. I heard her squeal her delight. I heard them laugh—his, a rumbling bass, hers, a light tinkling broken by funny snorts.

As I listened, I wondered how the same man could be a loving father and a husband who'd casually broken my heart, again, this morning.

As I listened, I wondered if I ever really knew that man.

We started dating based on a lie. Sort of.

I was sixteen, a naïve church girl. He was nineteen, odd, gangly, and painfully introverted. We were matched as a prank masterminded by Tonse, his elder brother. We only knew the truth at our wedding, years later, when Tonse bragged about it while giving his speech as the best man. The way Tonse told it, he had tried unsuccessfully to get Ken to be more social and get a girlfriend, until the day he finally sussed that Ken had been smitten by me for years.

Before then, our fathers were professors in the Rivers State University, and we grew up in the quiet, tree-lined streets of the lecturers' quarters. Our families also attended the same chaplaincy church in the university where I sang in the choir. Though we weren't friends, I was classmates with Ngo, their younger sister, all through secondary school at FGGC Calabar, and it became a thing, on visiting days, for our parents to carpool or, if my parents couldn't visit, to send hers with food and provisions. Ken usually accompanied his parents on those visits, though I could swear the boy was dumb because he never spoke (although I would hear later that visiting days were one of the few things he appeared enthusiastic about—and this was what Tonse remembered and figured him out years later).

So Tonse enlisted Ngo's help to thread us together. At the time, Ngo and I were in our first years in different universities, Ken was already in his final year in my university, and Tonse was a junior doctor. I remember thinking it strange that during holidays when we were all back home on campus, Ngo suddenly seemed friendlier, sought me out, dragged me to their house almost every day, and involved the reticent Ken in our conversations. Many times, she asked Ken to walk me home, excusing herself with claims of tiredness, unexpected periods, and sudden illnesses.

We started from there. There was no now-we're-officially-dating moment, no kissing or holding hands till a few weeks before our wedding, and yes, no sex. People wondered how we coped, but we were two callow kids who were a bit scared, and we didn't miss what we never had. And looking back, it was still intimate without the sex. We bonded over books and video games (he taught me how to play, but I soon became good enough to always beat him in *FIFA 99* and finish him in *Mortal Kombat*). His first letters to me were the short comic strips he drew, with me as an athletic heroine defeating super villains. Then there was karaoke—their father had returned from a seminar abroad with a VCD player with a built-in karaoke function and two karaoke VCDs: *ABBA's Greatest Hits* and *Pop Hits of the '90s*. Because I lived to sing (bathroom star, soprano in the church choir), I hungrily took to karaoke like a piglet to a teat. Inevitably, I dragged Ken with me. It turned out he had a decent alto, and one of my favourite memories was one evening when he shed his reticence and surprised his family by singing "Fernando." And as I watched him, my heart quickly filled and spilled over, and I couldn't turn it off.

We talked—stripped and unravelled before each other, metamorphosed, and grew together. With him, the usually unspoken words in my head finally escaped into sharp-tongued wit. He was still quiet, but with me, he slowly steeled into a self-assured man. And we became almost inseparable, a rare sky-sea merge with no horizon.

We waited till we were married and laughed as we bumbled through the early days of discovering sex together till we found our rhythm. Lota was born two years into our marriage. Ken came to the operating theatre straight from the offshore rig, still in his coveralls. By then, I'd been in labour for eighteen hours. They sterilised him, and he joined me for the next five hours, through my screaming and cursing, the shit and the blood, till Lota came out, fists clenched like she was ready to fight the world. And Ken began sobbing, and I was startled because I'd never seen him cry. And Tonse, the doctor who had just delivered Lota, signalled for a nurse to take him out of the room. But he refused to leave, and Tonse said he'd let him stay if he cut the noise. A compromise was reached. He became quiet, but his tears streamed strong. He held my hand and smoothened my hair and watched as his brother carefully stitched my tear.

Now, I'm remembering that day as I'm on the phone with Ken. He's been offshore for a week, and he calls every day with his company's satellite phone. He's still apologising for the girl and our last conversation. There's this pause of expectation, and I realise he must have asked me a question I hadn't heard. I wait for him to ask it again, but he doesn't. Instead, he soft sighs. "Tell me what I have to do to make this right."

I'm numb. "Nothing, Kenwi. There's nothing you can do."

For a moment, we notice this was probably the first time I'd called him Kenwi, which was what non-family called him—he'd always been Ken to me.

He says, "We've got to get past this somehow."

I shake my head before I realise he can't see me. I want to say that for my sanity, I needed to get past this, but I couldn't. That I was trying to break the surface, but all the world's millstones were garlanded around my neck. That I didn't know how to be or what to be anymore. I want to say these things, but when I open my mouth, other words escape.

"I'm sorry, Kenwi. I can't be with you anymore."

Kenwi

Hey 8:28 p.m.

Tamara reads your message on Facebook Messenger immediately. She waits for an hour before she responds.

what do u want? 9:32 p.m.

You type, edit, and delete three times before you finally send, **I want to apologise. For the way I ended things between us. I should've been respectful. And kinder. I'm sorry. 9:45 p.m.**

u don't have to apologise, ur marriage & family come first. i was just the sidechic 10:17 p.m.

You're more than that, and you know it.
You're my friend. 10:18 p.m.

not anymore 10:20 p.m.

You met Tamara at work five months ago. On a blustery morning with the ocean throwing a violent strop, you noticed the chopper touch down gingerly on the helipad and four people jump out, a girl leading the way, unbowed by the gale, like she was Jesus about to hush the storm. About an hour later, Jollett, your immediate boss and the number-one man on the platform, summoned you to his office. There were three young men and the girl, all dressed in coveralls. She was rangy with short hair and an audacious spirit. Jollett introduced them as the new graduates employed by Imperial Oil as assistant subsea engineers. They were all to report to you indirectly, as you are the senior toolpusher, and there were two other levels between you and them. You realise that the girl was the first woman in a technical position on the platform. The other woman, matronly and caustic, worked in admin as the head of catering. Jollett told Tamara, "I guarantee that at many times, you'll feel that being a woman here is like being the only woman in a men's prison. But it's the job you chose. You're one of the boys now. No special treatment here. But he," Jollett pointed at you, "will keep everyone in line and make sure they don't trouble you."

Working brutal twelve-hour shifts every day in small spaces in the middle of the Atlantic can lead to many things, few of them good. There was a gym, small movie room, and a games room, which most guys were too knackered to use. Cabin fever, stir craziness, and sex starvation were common. You assigned Tamara to a room by herself, and on her first night, there were frantic knocks on her door from unknown men. She told you about it the next day. After issuing an email warning to everyone on the platform, you reassigned her to the room adjacent yours (moving out the four guys who were already there) and gave her a megaphone. Because there was internet connection but no signal for mobile phones, you friended each other on Facebook—in lieu of text messages was the excuse.

After work, a pattern of messaging each other on Facebook quickly developed. It started with talking about work—how she was coping, all that crap. Then it turned personal—dreams, secrets, and fears. Your chats looped from late at night to the early hours of the morning. The conversations flowed easily and quickly turned to a flood that swept you away and tore off the mask you hadn't realised you wore. (You would wear another mask during work hours when you hardly spoke to Tamara.)

By the fifth day, Skype replaced Facebook Messenger. And the first time you saw each other on the screens of the laptops, both half-dressed, you both knew. On the tenth day, with the air choked with longing, she asked to be excused so she could pleasure herself privately. You heard yourself, in a thickened voice, tell her that you didn't mind watching. She shrugged and held your eyes on the screen as she started, as she watched you take off your clothes and join her, till you groaned and spurted, and she rode the sight and sounds of you till her eyes glazed and she burst.

The rules were set quickly. Apart from Skype sex, there was no physical contact when you were both on the platform; it was too risky. Two weeks later, you shipped out together along with other people. The chopper dropped everyone at Imperial Oil's Port Harcourt Base, and you retrieved your car from the carpark while Tamara got into a taxi. No one guessed that outside the base, you followed the taxi to Tamara's apartment, where as you ran up the stairs to her door, it opened because she was already waiting for you behind it. You would spend two days there before you went home.

i hope things are now settled at home for you 10:25 p.m.

No. 10:25 p.m.

don't worry, she will forgive u 10:27 p.m.

I don't think so. She says she wants to leave. 10:27 p.m.

what? fr? 10:27 p.m.

Yes. 10:28 p.m.

wow. im so sorry 10:29 p.m.

Like I said earlier, I'm sorry too. 10:30 p.m.

its ok ♥ 10:34 p.m.

and we r still friends ☺ 10:35 p.m.

can u convince her not to leave? 10:35 p.m.

You think carefully before you type your answer. You read it and exhale. You send. **Honestly, I don't know. I fear that her mind is made up. 10:37 p.m.**

"You broke your halo, bro. Now you're just like the rest of us," Tonse says.

"Gloat all you want."

"I'm not gloating. Actually, I'm a bit sad."

"Why?"

Tonse frowns as he carefully measures ground coffee into the paper filter in the basket of his coffeemaker. It's almost four a.m., and you are sitting in his kitchen. He's up because he's got a caesarean scheduled for early that morning. You're up because your body clock is still on offshore time. You're in his house because you had nowhere else to go. After Wobia said she was leaving, you tried, unsuccessfully, to change her mind. You were offshore at the time, and it was hard to talk—you had to use one of the satellite phones that was shared with everybody, and there was a queue behind you of men who also wanted to make calls. You managed to negotiate a compromise—she wouldn't leave the house (because of Lota and because you were hardly around anyway). It made more sense for you to leave, or rather not come back. So you stayed on the rig for five weeks, more than the maximum you are allowed. Eventually, Jollett insisted that you go back on shore. You landed in Port Harcourt and went straight to the house, but Wobia had changed the locks. You saw her car parked outside, but she refused to open the door when you rang the bell. She also refused to answer your calls. You ended up in Tonse's house, where if his wife, Kokoma, was surprised to see you, she didn't act it. That was two days ago.

The fragrant aroma of the coffee hits you, and you both inhale. Tonse smiles. "Kenyan AA coffee. An ex-patient always gifts it to me."

Knowing Tonse, you wonder if the ex-patient is also an ex or current girlfriend. But you don't ask. He pours the coffee into mugs. "You know, weirdly, I was proud of you because you were not like me. I was proud that you were different . . . better." He winked. "Don't tell anyone I said this. It'll mess up my reputation as a lady-killer. Cream? Sugar?"

"Yes, both."

He sighs. "But if you were going to walk down this road, bro, you should have come to me for advice first."

"Ha! You?"

"I know things, you know?"

"Oh yeah? So, what would you have told me? How to hide it better so I wouldn't get caught?"

He shakes his head. "Every man gets caught, eventually. Some don't know they've been caught. No. I'd have told you not to do it."

Now you're surprised. "Really?"

"Yes." He hands you a steaming mug. "I have this theory. Generally, there are two types of married men who have affairs. For context, I'm talking about men who want to keep their marriages, notwithstanding whatever they get up to. First, there are men like me—so-called womanisers. With us, it's either fun or transactional. Sure, we rack more numbers, but the important point is, it rarely gets serious, and emotions seldom come into it. Then there are men like you. The good guys. Men who can't just cheat and move on. No. It's got to mean something. You say you never planned to cheat, it just happened. But either that's bullshit or you just weren't paying attention because it started with the emotional affair before it got sexual. Needy for relationships, you guys go in hard with your heart—all naïve, narcissistic, and stupid. Start relationships that are doomed to end in heartbreak because now you love your wife, and you love your girlfriend too. You won't cheat as many times as we do, but compared to us, your team has a worse cumulative effect on marriages." He sips his coffee. "So yeah, if you'd asked me for advice, I'd have said, no, don't do it. Because you're not a womaniser. Because you don't understand or respect the game, and you can't play it right. Because you'll get caught and screw up your marriage. And because no matter how much you think you're crazy in love with Tamara, you're sane enough to never give up Wobia and Lota for her."

It takes a moment for you to respond. "I think your theory is nonsense. And for the record, I've moved on. I've broken up with Tamara."

"I've broken up with Tamara." Tonse sneers as he mimics you. "Oh yeah? I bet you still exchange calls and messages daily, asking how each other's day went and shit, right?"

You look away and don't answer.

"I bet he still does."

Startled, you both turn to see Kokoma at the door of the kitchen in her dressing gown. She walks in, pats your shoulder in greeting, and gives Tonse a customary quick kiss. Her smile remains inscrutable.

"Please make me some of that . . . special coffee," she says to Tonse. "No cream. No sugar."

Wobia

"If you're going to ask me to forgive Ken, don't."

Kokoma smiled. "No, I wasn't going to ask you that."

She had spent that Saturday with me. She'd come just after

dawn with two big bowls of afang and egusi she had cooked and brought from her house. Then after I bathed Lota, she charmed her unruly hair into beautiful twists, muttering all the time that she wished she had a daughter to practice her hair-making skills on (she had three sweet but boisterous boys, whom she ruled with an iron hand). After, she took us to see a movie and get some ice cream. When we returned home, Lota had fallen asleep in the back of the car. I carried her to her room, and we settled down in the living room to talk. That was the first time she mentioned Ken.

"I resent that people expect me to forgive him. It's taken for granted that I should, like I have no choice really." I sing-sang an impression. "It happened just this once, dear. Don't overreact."

"Ngo said that?"

"Yes." I shook my head. "And my mum too. Ngo also said that other men are worse."

"True, but you didn't marry other men."

"Finally! Somebody understands this. Call me naïve, but if I'd married any other man, I wouldn't have had the same expectations I had for Ken." I sighed. "You know, I've already forgiven Ken. Honestly, I have. But . . ." I groaned. "How do I cope with the pain? Have you dealt with something like this? How did you do it?"

Kokoma smiled. "Let's just say, I knew the type of man Tonse is before we got married. So my expectations were different."

"If you don't mind my asking, what do you do when you catch him?"

"In the early days, he was a bit sloppy, and I found out a few. I felt so disrespected that I played my equalizer."

"What's that?"

"It's complicated to explain. First, you need to understand the power you have over a man who truly loves you and has given himself to you. You know his core, the thing that contains his essence, the place of his biggest fears and insecurities. You hold it in your hands every day, nurse, and nurture it. An equalizer is basically you holding a knife to it. Cut wisely. Do you nick, slash, or saw through his soul so deep that he bleeds out? It's up to you how you use your power. It's different for every man. For Tonse, I told him that I slept with my ex in revenge after I found out about his girlfriends."

My hands flew to my mouth to stop it, but the loud gasp had already escaped. "You slept with your ex?"

Half smiling, she gave me a cryptic, "What do you think?"

I gasped again. "How did he take it? What happened? Did he throw you out?"

Her laugh was a beautiful, pearly thing. "That's impossible. He's not that kind of man, and we both knew we can't function without each other. Plus, he understands the game. Long story short, eventually we talked, cried, forgave, had make-up sex, and everybody promised to be of good behaviour. He still carries on sometimes, but he's smoother now, so there's no disrespect. I always know sha."

"How?"

"Because his phone is always clean. I know those times when he works extra late or showers me with more attention and gifts than usual. I know because I know the man I love." She patted my arm. "Some say you only know true love when you've loved the unlovely, the imperfect. So perhaps it's better that you now see Ken's feet of clay."

"Love is shit."

"Sister, we can't survive without shit."

We were chuckling when I blurted out, "Do you swallow?"

Kenwi

You'd been spooning her, and you wake when she pulls away and leans half up on an elbow. You run your hand down her naked back, touch the birthmark under her right shoulder. She reaches behind, strokes your thigh. Without turning to look at you, she says, "It's four thirty a.m. You've got to go."

"What?"

"You need to leave. I don't want Lota to see you here."

"This is crazy." You're sitting up on the bed now.

"She believes you're offshore and will be there for a long time. I don't want her to see you this morning, and you won't be here when she gets back from school. It'll confuse and hurt her." She swings off the bed.

"I'll be here when she returns from school."

"What makes you think I want you here." She's standing, tousled hair, naked, arms akimbo. You're distracted by her breasts (perfect in their slight lopsidedness and size—not too big, not too small, just right for your hand) and the tuft between her legs. You feel a stirring between your legs.

"Wait. I thought . . ."

"You thought what? Because we had sex last night, you can move back in today? Look, I was horny, okay? Yes, we have our issues right now, but you're still my husband, and I believe I'm allowed to fuck you when I want." It's the first time you've heard her use profanity, and you sense that a side of her has been peeled off like an onion, and you're seeing a fresher, steelier Wobia. She backs you for a moment and bends to pick up your jeans from the floor.

The sight of her haunches and firm, rounded buttocks makes you go hard. She turns to face you and sees your erection. You catch her brief triumphant smile before she throws your jeans over your penis. "Get dressed."

"I'm not going anywhere."

"Please don't do this, Ken. I told you that we weren't going to get back together until I was ready." Her voice softens. "You agreed to give me time, remember?"

"It's been four months. How much longer?"

"I don't know."

"I miss you."

She sighs. "I miss you too."

Last night, after driving aimlessly to clear your head, you'd called her. You talked. Without prompting, you confessed some more truths—how you were still chatting with Tamara, until finally, you'd decided to cut that off, and how you'd convinced Jollett to reassign her off the platform, back to the Port Harcourt Base. Sometime during this conversation, you'd found yourself parked outside the house. She'd allowed you in. Lota was asleep and hadn't stirred when you knelt beside her bed, hugged her, and breathed her in. Your eyes welled when you stood, and instinctively, Wobia had reached for your face and wiped a tear with her thumb. The lost tenderness threw both of you, and the next moment, you were in the bedroom, tearing off clothes and making love as if it would be the last time.

"I'm sorry, Wobia."

"I know. And I love you too, Ken."

You both smile. She touches your cheek. "Now, quickly take a shower and leave."

Fifteen minutes later, you are sitting in your car, but you can't bring yourself to drive. You are hollowed out, desolate. You realise a truth so profound, it breaks your heart—you've lost the Wobia you knew, and though this new Wobia will love you, it will be a cold, jaded thing, a sorry substitute for the life force her love was to you. You need the old Wobia, and it would take a miracle to bring her back.

So, lost, you lower your head and begin to pray.

"River"*

Jon was wearing your shirt on the day he died.

You remember the shirt. Burgundy. Thick cotton. Long sleeves. He'd passed by your house months or weeks before, stayed for some days, and took the shirt with him. Knowing how pernickety you were, he promised to return it soon. Knowing Jon, you accepted that soon meant *whenever* or *maybe*.

You ironed the shirt for him that morning. He'd spent the night in your house with his girlfriend, Biboye. You gave up your mattress for them, and you slept on cushions on the floor. Exams started the next day. The plan was they'd go to school and continue reading for exams. You preferred to revise at home. You didn't discuss if he could come back to your place that night. You didn't have to. Your home was his, and he could go and come as he pleased. You wish he came home that night.

You remember bringing them breakfast that morning, but you can't remember what they ate. They left with him smiling, that familiar and mischievous thing.

---

* Written under the influence of "River" by Leon Bridges

The next time you see Jon, he's not smiling. He's not wearing your shirt. He's in a black suit, stiff, lying straight, with one leg bent ever so slightly. His skin is waxy, and there's cotton in his nostrils. All-night open-casket wake. All night, people beg him to wake. All night, you sit next to him, talk to him. Then morning comes, and they bury him. Through it all, you ugly cry your eyes out.

You don't know it then, but you'll never stop crying.

1996.

You've tried therapy.

It hasn't worked.

You think it hasn't worked because to identify your demons and appreciate Jon's story fully, first, the therapists have to understand confra and confra culture, especially in the '90s in Nigeria. And they haven't. That's your theory, unscientific as it is, and you're sticking with it.

The last therapist you saw was in London. In 2016. During your MBA year. He was a reedy man with glasses who worked with the university.

You tried to explain confra to the man. You started with the simplest analogy—confras are gangs, just based mainly in some Nigerian universities. You didn't want to talk about names, so you used colours and symbols—Reds, Blacks, Yellows, Whites, Birds, Greens.

But the man didn't understand.

You knew he didn't understand because he asked shit like, "If you knew it was wrong, as you said you did, why did you join?"

You asked him if he really understood human nature or masculinity or if he knew why from the beginning of time, boys were drawn to wars knowing they'd die.

He mumbled something trite about toxic masculinity and the need to open up and show emotion, yen-yen-yen.

You realised he was an idiot.

You met Jon in 1993 during your undergrad.

You were both Jambites on a long queue for some registration process for first years. You remember that he and some other guys cracked jokes, impromptu entertainment for everyone, to pass the time. He tried to chance you on the queue, and you didn't let him, and he laughed like, *No hard feelings?* There were none. You got talking and quickly discovered that you were both doing the same course, both seventeen. You moved to the next registration queue as friends. It was that simple.

The list for hostel accommodation came out, and you were not assigned to the same hostel, but Jon wasn't having any of it. With you in tow, he went to have a word with the relevant admin people, including a Reverend Father (Jon was Catholic, and he played his ex-seminary secondary school and I'm-considering-the-priesthood cards). They were all strangers, but he persuaded them somehow, and they reassigned him to your hostel. You got the same room, and on the hostel list you wrote your names, one after the other. You would write your names like that—on attendance sheets and various school lists—for three years. Till he died.

You were an unlikely pair. You are the only child of your parents, used to having your own way, unused to sharing, introverted like it was a religious duty, fastidious about your clothes and things to the point where you couldn't leave your room with your bed unmade. Jon broke all that. He was free-spirited, messy, the baby in a family of five, charming like a smiling child. You met and were adopted into each other's families, completing the transition from friendship to brotherhood. Bromance before the word became a thing.

He was so full of life that he even tried to live vicariously through you. Like the times before Biboye, when he'd introduce you to a girl but call you aside and, dead serious, say crazy shit like, "I want to straff this girl, but I can't because I'm already with her friend. So, I want you to do it. Because you're my bro, if you do it, it'll be like I'm the one who did it. Ah tink you understand?" You didn't understand. But you did it anyway. And after you were done and he found out, you were always bemused by his unbridled joy.

Girls' hostels, lectures, parties—you rolled almost everywhere together. It was not surprising that you rolled into confra together.

Confra.

When you gained admission into the university, your parents, like everybody else's parents, warned you not to join a confra. They didn't call it confra; they used the government name—secret cult. Everyone knew of at least one sad story—of boys who had been injured or killed, arrested, or expelled because of confras. Because civilians mostly hear about confras when there's a war or some violence, they usually assume confra guys are all gangbangers.

They're wrong.

Confra housed everybody.

There was space for gangbangers and choir boys and armed robbers and poets and thieves and rappers and rapists and vigilantes. Conmen thrived with philanthropists, shayo men with teetotallers, politicians with activists, groove men with nerds. For young men in an unconscious search for identity and brotherhood, part of confra's appeal was this—whatever they were or aspired to be, there was already a confra guy, mentorlike, ahead on that path. So, a sensitive and thoughtful teen with an interest in philosophy would find an older confra guy with the mannerisms of a librarian, who befriends him, lends him his copy of de Beauvoir's *The Second Sex*, tunes him to Kant and Nietzsche, while quietly extolling the benefits of blending Red or Black or Yellow. You saw this happen.

Confra was a culture. You and Jon were into hip-hop culture, gangster culture. Confra sucked you in.

1994.

You're both eighteen. Because you know everything, you believe you'll be eighteen forever. Wannabe gangster, you see and resee *Goodfellas*, you read and reread *The Godfather*. You rap, listen to rap—"Hip Hop Hooray." You come down from *The Chronic*—call weed indo. You drink Guinness and Fanta—pretend it's gin and juice. *Juice*—see and resee Pac as Bishop. "Juicy"—Notorious. Walkman and Afro on your head. "Nappy Heads." Friday dates. Sex. *Doggy Style*. You dig your style. Timberlands and baggy jeans—you're fresh to death, killing it. You think you're cool.

But the confra guys appear cooler, ice-cold sef. They're older, have more baffs, better collections of music. One guy even has cable in his BQ room where you go to watch *Yo! MTV Raps*. They share their music and their smokes. They invite you to parties. They introduce you to older, finer girls—girls who should be out of your league but who pay you attention, laugh at your jokes, and even flirt because you're with confra guys. All the while, the confra guys pay you compliments, whisper in your ears, tell you they'll be honoured if you blend into their confra if you choose Red over Yellow or Black over White.

Every confra headhunted you and Jon. Because he was friendlier, they talked to him more. Because you were always together, it was understood without words—you would join a confra as a duo or not at all.

And that's how it happened. They convinced Jon, and Jon convinced you. Truth is, you didn't really need much convincing. It had been a long time coming.

So, one night in 1994, you and Jon were initiated into the biggest confra in your university.

You were in. You were made men.

And everyone knew because, frankly, there were no real secrets in secret cults. Perhaps if you and Jon were quieter, nerds even, your covers would have lasted a lot longer. But you fancied yourselves as guy-men, so you were out there, cocky, strutting and shakara-ing like peacocks. And because you knew everything, you believed you were invincible. At first you enjoyed it—the fact that everybody seemed to know your names, the respect from other confra guys and civilians, the way girls stopped forming and started listening.

But it unravelled quickly for you.

It started when you liked a girl. A Jambite you'd seen around. Finally, coincidentally, you met her at a business centre where you both went to make photocopies. You talked, walked her to her hostel. On the way, you found she was a hip-hop head too, a big fan of A Tribe Called Quest. You both impromptu-rapped the first verse of "Check the Rhime," you as Q-Tip, she as Phife. She was perfect. For about thirty blissful minutes, you stood in front of her hostel, talking music and laughing. You were high and puppy-loved-up when you left her (after agreeing on a date in two days). The next day, she sent you a message. It came through her cousin, an older guy in your confra. He told you she was scared of you, and she'd only indulged you with her company because she felt you'd threaten her if she didn't. Shocked and righteously indignant, you told him to tell her you weren't one of those guys who use their confra status to threaten girls to date or sleep with them. He said he understood, but as a sign of respect to him and to make her feel comfortable, you should stay away from her. You stayed away (you'd reconnect with her later, but that's another story).

That experience cut you. And it was an eye-opener. You realised other confra men and civilians didn't really respect you; they feared you, loathed you. At first, you struggled to process this. It wasn't that you needed people to love you—after all, you weren't a politician. It was just that you couldn't stomach the idea of people being fake to you because of fear; you preferred that they were honest with whatever emotion they felt. But that was almost impossible.

You started to notice other things.

Like how, while they preached brotherhood among members, your confra was run by a clique of guys who seemed more interested in lining their pockets with the membership dues everyone paid. And other cliques waited impatiently by the sidelines for their shot at power and turn at the trough.

You also noticed you couldn't relate with confra's warped sense of mass brotherhood. The idea, the ideal, was that all members of your confra were your brothers. You were supposed to share what you had with them, be ready to go to war for them. You had done that for Jon and a few guys in your clique whom you considered friends. But you weren't going to bleed for some asshole you didn't really know or like just because he was in the same confra as you. And there were many assholes in confra—small-minded but big bullies, always first to start trouble.

Screwface was one of those assholes in your confra. He called himself Screwface after the villain in the then-popular Steven Seagal movie. An irascible and irksome guy, he got into an argument and a jostle with some other guy from another confra over turns to use the bathroom in one of the hostels or some childish shit. It escalated into a shoving match, words were thrown, and suddenly, word spread that there was a possible war with the other confra. While Jon and your other guys were pumped to defend Screwface from the "disrespect," quietly, you told Jon that you thought the whole thing was stupid, and Screwface wasn't worth defending because truth be told, he probably needed to get smacked occasionally. Jon didn't agree, and that was the beginning of a temporary crack in your relationship. Screwface's wahala would have resulted in a longer war if not for the intervention of peacemakers from both confras. Before the peace was made though, two guys fought publicly and were later expelled; and the quieter battles resulted in injuries on both sides. Screwface wasn't scratched.

You learned two lessons from this.

First, confra trouble, when it came, didn't pick out the idiot who poked and provoked it—it came for everybody.

More importantly, you also learned that confra was bullshit.

1995–96

You tried to explain your disillusionment to Jon, but he didn't understand—yet. Plus, at the time, he and your clique were beginning to grow influential in your confra. Power was close; your words sounded like gibberish.

You began to pull away—gradually.

Resignation was not an option. The only way out of confra was graduation from school. You still paid your dues, but that was about it. You stopped partying and hanging out with your confra guys except with Jon and the few friends in your clique. You refused to get a place at school, choosing instead to commute from home every day. You refused to tap anybody to convince them to blend. Some younger guys from your neighbourhood, guys who looked up to you, got into your school. You told them quietly not to blend into your confra. They nodded their agreement. But confra culture was too strong and seductive—so, one by one, they all blended. Then they smiled sheepishly at you when you found out. You smiled back like, *No wahala,* but inside, you shook your head and sighed. They'd learn.

Finally, Jon learned.

Love taught him, cured him. He met Biboye, and they started dating. She was good to him, good for him. His priorities changed. He became a gentler, smarter man. He stopped sleeping around. He'd been slipping with his academics, and he refocused. He was always a smiling guy, but for the first time, you noticed that his smiles came from a peaceful, sunny place within, and he glowed. You'd tease him about it, and he'd smile some more and talk about marrying Biboye as soon as possible. Crazy talk because he was nineteen. Crazy too because you hoped it would happen.

More importantly, love opened his eyes to confra's absurdities and monstrosities. And like you, he withdrew from active participation.

But trouble and wars didn't discriminate between active and passive members. The wars were usually short, typically over in a week or two, after cool heads intervened. Wars were occasional events, sandwiched between long periods of fragile peace. The thing with wars was, many times they started with little or no warning. This was a time when there were no mobile phones, when news was spread by word of mouth, and guys who didn't hear on time got ambushed.

So you and Jon developed a system for avoiding trouble. You were careful wherever you went, always watched people around, looked for suspicious faces. You walked into rooms and immediately noted all the available exits. You started sitting only at the ends and never in the middle of any row. You stopped sitting with your back to doors. You were paranoid as hell.

It was nonsense.

Despite your best efforts, you walked into an ambush once. You'd reconnected with Girl-Phife, who was scared of you a year before. You were taking it slow, making sure she was comfortable, hoping to date her. On a cool evening, you strolled with her to the Staff Club to buy suya. Unknown to you, war had broken out between your confra and the Whites an hour before. You noticed five Whites at the same time they saw you, and something in their faces told you this was trouble. As they walked towards you menacingly, you realised they were blocking the only exit. You did the only thing you could. Your shirt was untucked, and you put your hand under it near one side of your waist, a gesture to show that you were carrying a gun. They stopped. You exchanged hard stares, and slowly, you walked through them, one hand still hidden under your shirt, the other holding the girl, out of the Staff Club.

You were lucky that day.

You weren't carrying a gun.

And years later, the girl would be your wife. But that's another story.

You learned another lesson. Getting ambushed was down to the lottery of bad luck and little else.

Jon's luck ran out on the day he left your house wearing your shirt.

They said, that night, he stopped by a room in the Boys' Hostel to shoot the breeze with Obari, one of your mutual friends. The room was frequented by your confra guys. It was full of them that night.

Till today, no one knows who in the room was the target of the hit. It didn't matter anyway.

They said there were two hitmen. The room had only one door. The hitmen appeared at the door.

They said Jon was the first to sense what was about to happen.

They said he charged at the door, at the hitmen, shoved past them.

They said Jon's action disconcerted the hitmen so they didn't kill as many as they could have in the room.

They said the hitmen shot and killed only Obari inside the room.

Only?

They said the hitmen shot Jon as he ran.

They said he ran with the bullets in his back to the room of another mutual friend, where he lay on the floor heaving, bleeding.

They said eventually, they managed to get him into a car to take him to a hospital. The information greyed out at this point.

They said all these things to you because you weren't there. You were home, preparing for your exams the next day. If you'd been there, you'd have visited that room with Jon. Maybe you'd have been shot too. Maybe not.

The next day, one of your friends came to your house just before dawn. He told you Obari was dead, and Jon had been shot, but he didn't know how injured he was or the hospital where he was being treated.

Your exam was scheduled for the afternoon. You hadn't finished your revision. You went to school immediately.

As you walked through the gates, the first person you saw was Biboye's brother.

You ask which hospital Jon was admitted to get treatment for his injuries.

He looked at you, incredulous. "Jonathan don die. You never hear?"

2018

Confras are still in Nigerian universities. Confras are also outside universities for guys who have graduated. Apart from the ones who run criminal rings (for drugs, organised crime, and prostitution) in Italy and other parts of Europe, confras are more social clubs at this post-university stage. They hold public conventions, organise lectures, donate to charities, throw parties, and even organise wholesome family-events stuff. You see ex-confra or old confra guys everywhere. A sizeable number are in politics, an ex-Black hitman is a pastor (you recognised his face on a poster advertising a crusade he was to preach in), an ex-White is a manager in your bank, and two ex-Reds are judges; most guys from that era are husbands and fathers now, living their lives, loving their families.

You wonder if they remember the old days and how they remember it—with nostalgia or shame or joy or guilt? You wonder if some carry scars like you. It's unlikely, you know, but you hope they are all good fathers. You've thought hard about this over the years. You remembered that all the premium assholes you knew in the old days, the guys who would easily stab someone when a slap or a telling-off or glare would have sufficed, had no or absentee fathers, and the calmer guys seemed to come from more stable homes. Your theory may be cliché and anecdotal, but it's based on your experience, and so you stick with it. So, sometimes, you pray that somehow, all ex-confra men become good fathers—so their sons don't repeat all the bullshit.

You're full civilian now. Gentrified. Married. Your sons ouch and aww instead of chei or kai. When the time comes, God willing, they won't attend schools where confras are a thing. You only battle in boardrooms now, polite skirmishes with money, not ego, as the prize. Many regard you as successful, and truth be told, you're thankful for your lot.

But you still cry for Jon.

Like bird shit, it comes without warning, always catching you by surprise. One minute, you're bobbing through life like most people, the next, the sudden sting of tears when you remember Jon. The tears have come at your sons' school during a meeting with one of their teachers. In the middle of a board meeting, when you were about to close a deal. On a plane back to Port Harcourt, where an airhostess caught your eye, assumed you feared flying, and patted your shoulder. When you hear random songs—as in, the songs don't even have to be sad sef—like that party in 2013 where you and your wife danced to Robin Thicke's "Blurred Lines" till you suddenly realised that Jon would never hear it, and the tears came.

You've developed a rapid-response system for when you're in public. As you feel the tears, you turn away, remove your glasses, pretend to dab your eyes with your handkerchief, pretend to clean your glasses. The moment passes. You're cool again.

You don't mind crying, really. It's just the inappropriateness of it all. When you're at home or somewhere private, you welcome the tears, let them flow till you're dried out. But they fill up quickly, again and again. In 2012, you read Eghosa Imasuen's *Fine Boys,* and the story was so coincidentally yours, it broke your heart again and fucked up your life for days. You ugly cried for the first time in a while. You never read the book again.

Your wife knows why you cry. Luckily, she knows when to hold you, when to talk to you, and when to leave you be. You're thankful for that.

Sometimes though, she reminds you, quietly, that you need to get help. You know you need help.

Your father died in '97, almost a year after Jon. Complications from a stroke.

You've not cried for your father. Almost twenty-one years later.

And it's not that you didn't love the man—you did, still do. And it's not for want of trying—you've tried as hard as you can. You are desperate to cry for your father. In your head, it will be the final act in your grieving process, so you can turn the last page and move on with the memories alone. But you can't. You know it's probably a silly thought, but sometimes, you feel like all your tears have been reserved for Jon, and no drop will be spared for your father, or anyone else, despite your wishes. So you're left with this uneasy feeling of unfinished business, ungrieved grief. You resent this because you're helpless and can't do anything to change it.

Fuck.

No one knows for sure who killed Jon and Obari.

Some said it was the Blacks. Some said the Whites. You heard your confra retaliated, equalised, and even went ahead. You heard three Whites were killed in UniPort and UniCal, two Blacks in UniPort and UniBen.

It didn't give you any comfort because you knew the game. The guys who died would not have known Jon or had anything to do with his death. They died because of the colours they'd blended into and because they won in the lottery of bad luck.

You almost feel guilty for your luck. You feel guilty about a lot of things.

The guilt is a monster that sits on your shoulder and cripples you. You feel it anytime you see Jon's family. Warm people, they've loved you more after he passed. But you don't know how to deal with their kindness. You think your presence, your existence, would always remind them of the son they lost. You feel guilt whenever you visit them, but you also feel guilt for not visiting them as often as you'd like. And it breaks your heart when, as you leave after a rare visit, they hug you and tell you to come again soon and not to be a stranger.

Your guilt extends to Biboye. She's married with kids now and runs a successful business. You went through the immediate aftermath of Jon's death and burial together, but soon after, you drifted. Conversations were reduced to perfunctory small talk. You realise now that like you, she grieved for a long time, probably still does. And you knew nothing of it. Maybe it was because you were dealing with your own shit, but now, you feel you should have asked her. You should have seen behind the "I'm-fine" masks you both wore. You should have helped her.

Maybe in doing so, you'd have helped yourself.

You need help.

You're confused about what you need help for. You don't want to stop thinking about Jon or have his memory erased from your mind. You're not sure you want to stop grieving. Maybe you need help for the ever-fresh, ever-ripe pain. You need help to finally grieve for your father.

Your wife suggested that you should talk to God.

You told her you'd prayed about it many times before, but nothing changed.

She pointed out that you struggle to identify and express your true feelings when you talk. She partly blamed it on you being an introvert and an only child.

She suggested you may open more if you wrote. She showed you a prayer journal she keeps. She let you read bits of it. They were her conversations with God, but they're not like any prayers you've seen or heard. You read about things you'd both gone through, past arguments you'd had, and you realise that many things had hurt her deeper than she admitted.

She gave you a similar notebook and urged you to write your thoughts, raw and unfiltered, just like hers.

You started writing last night. You wrote all through the night. You poured out everything—the words, the tears. The sheets in the notebooks were smudged, sodden. It was illegible in parts, there were many cancellations, and it was chock-full of typos. It also carried some profanity, but that was the most authentic way you could express yourself at those moments. It's messy, but it's the truth, as full as you've ever told it before.

You finished writing this morning. As you sip your fourth coffee, you hope that writing this story will help you.

You will wait to find out.

"Love's Divine"*

Is the man here?" JJ covers his mouth with his hand as he speaks like professional footballers on TV.

"What man?"

"The scout, abi agent."

Boma scans the sparse crowd. They're at No. Six Field in Port Harcourt's Old Township. "I don't know. But he said he'll come."

"And he wants more players?" It was the fifth time JJ had asked.

Boma nods and continues with his warm-ups.

JJ brisk-jogs on the spot, then does thirty jumping knee tucks. Usually, he did ten. He looks at the crowd when he finishes, hoping that somehow, he'll identify the unknown man if he sees him. The man, a Nigerian based in America, had come regularly during the last two weeks, a period when JJ's father had ordered him to stay away from No. Six Field because he was writing his WAEC exams. In that time, the man had said he was impressed with Boma and had offered to take him to America for trials with a Major League Soccer club. All Boma had to do was raise the two hundred fifty

* Written under the influence of "Love's Divine" by Seal

thousand naira needed to cover his registration fees to the man's agency and other administrative expenses. The MLS club would cover the costs of visas, travel, food, and board.

Recurring but unspoken thoughts play in JJ's head—he's a better footballer than Boma. Boma is a defender, a commanding centre-back, yes, but nothing more. JJ played across all attacking positions but preferably as a winger, a role where he performed his best magic, spellbinding crowds. Yes, sometimes his tricks didn't come off and his showboating could exasperate, but everybody loved a showman. JJ was confident that if the man watched him play, he'd offer to take him to America.

Coach-ay blows his whistle, the signal for everybody to get ready. Coach-ay, grey but wiry, is going to referee the game and coach both teams at the same time. It's his neighbourhood, his football club, and he does whatever he wants. The boys, all teenagers, are members of his club, and he'd divided them into two teams, eight-a-side, but to play on a full field to build their stamina. JJ's team is in the dull orange training bibs. Boma's team wears the fading, fluorescent green. Coach-ay shouts final instructions on tactics to both teams. "Orange, play three–three–one. Green, two–three–two. Let's go."

The game starts. JJ is on the left of Orange's midfield three. The early exchanges are frenetic but disjointed, typical of youth soccer. JJ waits for a chance to show himself.

Eventually, it comes. Green attacks Orange's goal, and JJ tracks back to defend but hangs at the edge so he can launch a fast counterattack if the opportunity comes. Then, an ungainly Orange defender hoofs the ball out. It wasn't intended as a pass, but it comes sailing towards JJ. He sticks a foot out and brings the ball down under his spell. With the ball close-controlled at his feet, he goes on an amazing run through three Green defenders, including Boma, feinting and dancing his way past them, nutmegging one, making the crowd gasp and cheer.

Now he's close to the penalty box. (Because No. Six Field is mainly sand, earth, and a few tufts of grass, the penalty box is pure conjecture.) The onrushing goalkeeper is almost on him. The Orange striker is on his right, screaming for him to square the ball. If he does, the striker has the easiest of tasks—pass into an open goal to score. Everyone expects him to take this option.

He chips the ball, scooping and looping it over the goalkeeper.

In the same movement, he's off, towards the corner, not looking at the ball, confirming the goal from the crowd's roar. For his celebration, he takes off his jersey and training bib, smacks his bare chest, screams his name, and jumps into a small group of seven spectators. They group hug him, bounce and jig with him, bedlam in a teacup, forgetting that they were strangers seconds ago. His teammates, except the striker, run to celebrate with him.

When it finally breaks and they return to the centre, Coach-ay jogs to him, his hand raised, and because there are no physical yellow cards, says, "Yellow card. For offing your shirt." Then he smiles. "Good goal. But next time, pass."

"How many did you score today?" Onis, his father, asks.

JJ moves the jollof beans around his plate with a fork but doesn't eat. "Two. Three assists."

"Great."

Grace, his mother, regards him. "Why the long face? You don't like your food?"

"Nothing. Food is nice."

"Then act like it. I didn't cook beans in the pressure pot for you to be morose over it."

His younger sisters, Anume and Saniye, giggle, and he glares at them across the dining table.

The agent hadn't come. The game of his life—two goals, three assists, dozens of mazy dribbles, a man-of-the-match performance—but the agent didn't show. He feared the man had returned to America; Boma had mentioned that he was in Port Harcourt for only a short time. He hadn't told his parents about the man. He sensed they wouldn't like the idea. They supported his football, especially his father, but they were clear that his education came first. They were not going to agree to his going to America for trials at sixteen if there were no guarantees that he would get a university education in the bargain.

"Justin."

JJ looks up at him. "Yes, Dad."

"We want to talk to you about something important," Onis says softly. "Later this night."

JJ notices his mother catch her breath, then exhale, as his father speaks. Then they exchange anxious looks. Suddenly, the air is heavy, and he's nervous. He nods. "Yes, Dad."

They wait till after dinner, after prayers, after his sisters are in bed. They meet in the living room. His parents sit on the couch opposite him, their favourite seat, in their favourite position—knees touching, interlocked hands. JJ sits, looking behind them to the shelf that held some family pictures. There are baby pictures of him, Anume, and Saniye, and a picture of his mother, beaming triumphantly, in her square academic cap and gown on the day of her convocation. There is also a picture of his parents at their wedding—a picture that caught the essence of their marriage. In it, his mother throws her head back and laughs, her hand flung round his father's shoulder; and his father leans towards her, and in his smile, one can almost hear the punchline of the private joke he'd just told her; and he, JJ, the seven-year-old page boy, looks at them, wide-eyed and baffled at the jokes that fly over him.

"My son," Onis begins. He is a quiet, perceptive man, who saves all his mischief and vulnerability for his wife. He's also miserly with his words, sparing no more than is necessary. "When we finish this conversation, always remember that I'm your father." Then he takes a deep breath and holds JJ's eyes.

"I am not your biological father."

Time stops.

"What do you mean you're not my father?"

"I'm your father. Just not your biological father."

"I don't understand."

But he was beginning to understand, to get the answers to the foggy, unformed, never-asked questions in his subconscious. Like why he looked different—taller, darker—than everyone in his family. Like why, unlike with Anume and Saniye, there were no baby pictures of him and Onis, a man who doted on his children; in their earliest picture together, he was three or four, a toddler. Like why he was named Justin after his maternal grandfather. And like why he didn't have an Engenni name like his sisters.

He repeats himself. "I don't understand." He looks at his mother. "How?"

"Oh, JJ," she whispers.

The blood pounds in JJ's head, and he rests it in his hands. It takes a long time before he speaks. "Who am I?"

Onis says, "You're Justin Awori. Future engineer or footballer, beloved son of Onis and Grace Awori, brother of Anume and Saniye."

JJ shakes his head. "You . . ." He hesitates. "You lied to me."

"You don't know the full story, JJ. It's complicated."

"What is my fa—." He sighs. "What is his name?"

"Dami," his mother replies. "Damiete Kuruye-Briggs."

Silence.

"So I have to change my surname?"

Onis speaks carefully. "When you become an adult, you can choose any name you want."

"Is he coming to take me away?"

"Ha!" His mother snorts. "No. He never wanted you." There was an edge in her voice.

"Why didn't he want me?"

Grace grimaces and sighs as her old wounds are reopened. "I don't know."

"Where is he?"

They exchange a quick glance. "He's dead."

He played his worst game.

It was still the same eight-a-side, full-field format, but he struggled to string simple give-and-go passes. He was dispossessed four key times, three of which directly led to goals for the Orange team, earning him hard stares and a bollocking from Boma and his other teammates (he was in Green this time, same as Boma). Up front, his dribbles, tricks, and stepovers didn't quite come off; the Orange goalkeeper pulled a series of spectacular saves, à la De Gea, and the one time JJ managed to round him, the angle was tight and his shot struck the post.

Then the fight.

He was leading a rare Green counterattack and had managed to slalom past two Orange defenders. There was a last Orange defender, but there was also a Green striker in space. All he had to do was pass. He tried to dribble past the defender, but the boy anticipated this and slide-tackled him, cleanly, knocking him off his feet and the ball off course from goal. They got up and chased the ball, but the defender got it first, and as he charged, the defender nutmegged him and slipped away. Humiliated, he caught up with the boy just as he cleared the ball upfield and kicked his hamstring. The Greens, still pissed at him for squandering yet another chance, left him alone in the ensuing fracas with the Orange defenders. Coach-ay got to the scene in time to see him throwing a wild punch (but didn't see the earlier punch at him that bust his lower lip). Coach-ay declared a red card for him and yellows for almost every Orange.

In Coach-ay's football club, one punishment for a red card was washing everybody's training bibs.

So, there he is, on the sideline, waiting for the game to end so he can take everyone's bibs home, sucking his broken lip, tetchy as a rabid dog.

"Terrible game for you, but you gonna do berra next time. Dun' worry ah-baw-rrit."

He turns to look at the man who has slipped in beside him. Apart from the accent, he has an I-just-got-back style written all over him—black baseball hat with *LA* on it, black *Black Lives Matter* T-shirt and ripped jeans, silver Jesus piece, and white sneakers.

"You JJ?"

JJ nods.

"You musta heard ah-baw me. I'm Jerry. The agent. Boma told me ah-baw you. You gat game, bro. You gat game."

JJ beams.

"How old are you?"

"Sixteen."

"Fo' real?" Jerry pulls a pleasantly shocked face. "You gat game like you eighteen or twenny. I can tell you gon' be a star. You wanna be a star, bro?"

JJ wanted to be a star.

Jerry smoothly explained the shortcut to stardom. He said he was a FIFA-licensed agent who specialised in getting teenage trialists into academies of soccer clubs in America and Europe and eventually on their way to the first teams. He reeled out names of boys he had worked with, whipped out his phone, and showed JJ pictures of Black boys, his clients, training in various clubs. He could get JJ in, but JJ needed to register with his agency first by paying a registration fee. He clarified that the fee was in dollars, which when converted to naira came up to just over two hundred fifty thousand, but because he liked JJ, he was willing to give JJ a discount and collect a flat two-fifty K. He said he preferred to collect the money in cash because although he was Nigerian, he'd been based in LA for the last twenty years and didn't have a Nigerian bank account. He asked JJ if he liked LA; and JJ (whose only trip outside Nigeria was to Ghana by road with Coach-ay's club for an invitational tourney) confirmed that he loved LA. Jerry explained that the president of LA Galaxy, a friend of his, had mentioned last week that their youth academy was looking for a flying winger, and he believed JJ fit the bill. He was certain he could get JJ on a plane to LA, all expenses paid, for them to check him out. But JJ had to register with his agency first, and this had to be done soon, as he was leaving Port Harcourt in a week.

JJ thinks quickly. He would have preferred going to Europe

where the standard was better and because he'd always dreamt of playing for Barça or Arsenal. But if LA Galaxy provided an immediate escape route from the sudden uncertainty in his life, then it was time for edited and new dreams.

JJ knows Onis and his mother won't agree to give him the money for the registration, but he hears himself say, "Don't worry. You'll get your money."

JJ goes to the future and sees his face when he's in his forties.

The man looks exactly like him—same height and dark skin, narrow, oblong face, high forehead and cheekbones, and wide lips—the only difference is that the man is fuller, has a beard with tiny grey flecks, and wears glasses.

The man looks at JJ in fascination and grins (they even smile the same). "My God, you look like Dami."

At this, his mother glares at the man while Onis remains stony-faced. They're on their couch, holding hands as always.

The man leans forward in his chair, raises his palms placatingly, and speaks to Grace and Onis. "My name is Diepriye Kuruye-Briggs. You can call me Priye. I'm the older brother of Damiete, Dami. First, I owe you several apologies. For disrupting your family now. I can't imagine how difficult this must be for you." He looks at Grace. "I apologise for how my family treated you years ago. I only found out about Justin recently."

"Your mother knew." Grace's voice quavers. "She knew when I got pregnant. She knew when Dami denied it. She helped Dami run to the UK and left instructions at your family house in GRA that they shouldn't let me in."

Priye winces. "I helped Dami run away. I just didn't know he was running away. Our father had died, and I began running our family's company in his place at the time. Dami was still in UniLag then. In his third year, he came to me suddenly and said he wanted to go to school in the UK immediately. I refused at first. I suggested that he should finish his last year, then go for a master's instead. But my mother put pressure on me, and I relented. I didn't know he was running from you." He sighs. "I understand you were in UniLag together?"

Grace nods.

He glances at her convocation picture on the shelf. "I'm happy you went back to school and finished." He smiles. Grace doesn't smile back. "If it's any consolation, Dami went to the UK but never finished school. Karma, eh?"

Grace allows herself a small smile.

"Dami had cancer and was ill for a while. Ten days before he died, he mentioned you and Justin. That was the first time I heard about you both. I also found out that my mother knew. Without airing my family's dirty linen any further, I will only say that my mother covered up a lot of Dami's misdeeds. I wish she hadn't." He sighs again. "I could have come earlier, but his last days were tough, and afterwards, I had to sort out the cremation and put his affairs in order."

"So, what do you want?" Onis asks.

Priye takes a deep breath. "My brother was not the best of men, but in the end, he tried, unsuccessfully, to right some of his wrongs. I'm here because he asked me to apologise to you." He looks at Grace. "And to you." He looks at JJ. "To be clear, he didn't expect forgiveness from you. He wanted you both to know that he regretted what he did, or didn't do, and he was genuinely sorry.

He wrote you these letters." He reaches in the inside breast pocket of his jacket and pulls out two envelopes. He drops them on the centre table. "I am also apologising on behalf of my family and my mother who's too ashamed to be here."

There is a heavy silence for a long moment till Grace says, "Is that all?"

"There's another thing. But I'm not sure this is the best time to mention it."

"What is it?"

Priye hesitates. "Dami left half of his shares in our family company to Justin and the other half to his wife. The company is doing well, and I will ensure that Justin gets his dividends at the end of the year. We also managed to set up a trust fund for Justin three days before Dami died. It's a modest amount, but I'm the trustee, and I know how to grow money. I think it's enough for his fees now if you want it, or if you prefer, he'll get a sizeable amount of money when he becomes an adult."

"God punish Dami."

"What?"

Grace yells her clarification. "I said, God punish Dami and his money. He will burn in hell. I begged him to support me, just to admit that he was the father, but the stupid boy thought I wanted to entrap and marry him because of your family's money. Because of him, I became the girl who was sleeping around, who didn't know who the father of her child was, a fallen woman." She stops, exhales, heaves. Her tone is softer, but the pain is still raw. "Where was this money at antenatal? Where was it during my caesarean and the five weeks JJ lived in the incubator at the neonatal ICU because he was a preemie? Where was Dami's money when JJ was two and fell down the stairs and fractured his arm?"

Now she speaks through gritted teeth, almost snarling. "Sixteen years later, you come to our house, sit in front of the man who has loved and raised JJ as his blood since he was three, and you insult us by talking about money as if we said we can't feed JJ or pay his fees."

She stands, grabs the envelopes from the centre table, and shoves them at him. "Please leave our house."

He knows that his mother's ATM card is in her black purse. The purse is in her big everyday handbag by her bedside. She's in the living room when he sneaks into his parents' bedroom. A few seconds later, he slips her ATM card in his pocket. Onis's card is harder to find because he doesn't keep a wallet. Quick check of his bedside drawer. No luck. Quick search of the shelves in the wardrobe. Not there. He's about to give up when he spots the trousers Onis wore yesterday hanging on the wardrobe door. Rifle through the pockets. Keys, driver's license. ATM card!

He leaves the house saying he's going for training. He hops on a bus on Aggrey Road and hops off near a bank of ATMs. There is a short queue. He waits in line, fidgety, chewing his nails.

It's his turn. He slots in his mother's card. He knows her PIN because she usually sends him with her card to make withdrawals for her. He checks her balance. N78,154.52. He removes her card and slots in Onis's. He doesn't know Onis's PIN, but he recalled that his mother let it slip once that it was Onis's birth year. Or was it her birth year? He tries Onis's birth year. Incorrect PIN. He tries his mother's birth year. Incorrect PIN.

He knows he has one more try, and if he punches the wrong

PIN, the card will be blocked for at least twenty-four hours. He blows his cheeks. He rubs his palms briskly. On a whim, he punches in his birth year, praying at the same time. Correct PIN! He shakes his fist in quiet celebration.

Onis's balance is N106,931.49. His heart sinks. There was no way he was going to raise the two-fifty K. He withdraws N100,000.00 from Onis and N75,000.00 from his mother. In the middle of it, he sees his reflection on a glass panel above the ATM. He can't look at himself, so he turns away. He listens to the gentle whirring as the machine counts the money. He is waiting for the last tranche of his withdrawals, N15,000.00 from his mother's account, when his phone rings. It's his mother. Then he remembers. Banks send notifications texts to their customers' phones when withdrawals are made with their ATM cards. His mother and Onis would have seen the withdrawals on their phones. Shit! Shit! Shit!

Suddenly, he needs to pee. He lets the phone ring out. She immediately calls again. He still doesn't answer. Then Onis calls. He ignores his phone. He manages to put it on meeting mode and slips it in his pocket. He hops on another bus, heading to Borokiri. His phone vibrates nonstop in his pocket all through the ride. The bus takes him up Churchill, and he gets off just after it goes past Captain Amangala Street.

Jerry is in a hotel in one of the side streets. It's a seedy place that smells of damp, marijuana, and failure. For a moment, he wonders why Jerry, an international man of football, a whole FIFA-licensed agent from LA, would stay in a place like this. The receptionist directs him to Jerry's room. The corridor leading here is dark and narrow, and he uses his phone to light the way.

Jerry cracks the door open a little at his third knock. He smiles when he sees JJ and opens the door fully. "Come in. Come in."

A half-dressed, skin-bleached-light-skinned woman sprawls on the unmade bed. Jerry introduces her as his assistant. JJ says good morning, and in response, she gives him a glance and returns to chewing gum loudly and watching a Nollywood movie on TV. Jerry wears a dirty once-white singlet and jeans. He looks different, and JJ realises why. Jerry's not wearing his baseball hat. He's balding, and his hairline had receded to the middle of his head, but weirdly, the rest of his hair is styled in a defiant Afro.

He points JJ to a hardback chair and sits on the edge of the bed. "You came at the right time. I'm leaving Port Harcourt this afternoon. You have my money?"

"Yes, but not all."

"How much?"

"One seventy-five."

Jerry sighs. "This is why I dun' wanna deal with no amateur. I only wanna deal with professionals. Your friend, Boma, has paid his money like a professional. In one month's time, he will be in Texas, doing trials with FC Dallas. But you . . ." He shrugs. "Is like you wanna play with your future." He pronounces it as *foo-shaw*.

"I'll come back when I have the complete money."

Jerry raises a hand. "Wait, I have a better idea. Give me what you have now. When you get the rest, call me. I'll send you my assistant's bank account number for you to pay the balance, okay?"

"Okay."

"Oya, bring the money." The American accent slips.

JJ gives him the money. He counts it carefully. The woman looks away from the TV and watches him.

Complete, he sighs. "Is only because I like you, JJ. Usually, I dun' do this." He wags a finger. "Next time, be professional, okay?" He stands, walks to the bedside table, and brings a file and some papers. "Let me give you receipt. Always ask for receipt when you pay money, okay? Especially if you still have a balance to pay. That way, nobody can cheat you." He starts writing. "What's your full name?"

"Justin."

"Justin who?"

JJ hesitates then says, "Justin Kuruye-Briggs."

"You want me to lend you seventy-five thousand naira?"

"Yes. You can take it from my trust fund. I'll pay it back."

From Jerry's hotel, he'd come straight to Priye's office. He looks at the pictures on the shelf behind Priye's desk. One catches his eye. It's of a family, father and mother seated, and three boys, who all looked uncannily like him, standing. The two older boys stood behind the parents, and the youngest boy stood between them, smiling impishly through one missing tooth and holding the father's walking stick aloft.

Priye catches his glance. "That was us." He smiles. "Dami is the one holding the walking stick." He leans back and steeples his fingers. "Why do you want seventy-five thousand naira?"

JJ tells him. He leaves nothing out, including the money he stole from Onis and his mother, which he planned to pay back. He passes Jerry's receipt across the desk.

Priye listens silently and studies the receipt, his face deadpan. When JJ finishes, Priye says, "Give me a few minutes." He turns to his laptop and types softly. Eventually, he stops typing and stares at JJ.

"I have two bits of interesting news for you. One, there is no such thing as a FIFA-licensed agent. Agents are licensed by the football associations of their countries. I have sent an email for someone to investigate for me, but I am willing to bet that this Jerry Lasisi fellow is not licensed by the NFF or the football association in the US.

"Secondly, LA Galaxy does not use agents to recruit players for their academy. The youth academy page on their website specifically says so. See." He turns the laptop's screen to face JJ.

JJ reads it for himself. He pulls out his mobile and calls Jerry's phone. It's switched off.

"I bet he has also checked out of the hotel by now," Priye says softly. "Jerry scammed you."

As JJ's face crumples and the tears roll, Priye says, "This is what I'll do for you. I'll give you one hundred seventy-five thousand naira. The money you took from your parents. Return it to them. Apologise for taking it. They don't need to know you paid their money to Jerry. They also don't need to know I gave it back to you. But understand—this is a loan, and you must pay it back. We'll discuss a payment plan later. It's not that I can't give you one seventy-five K. I can, but if I do, you won't understand that there's always a consequence for your every act of foolishness. I won't indulge you like my mother indulged Dami. Do you understand?"

JJ nods.

"Good. Do we have a deal?"

"Yes."

"Splendid." Priye picks up the receipt. "Now this." He shakes his head as he tears it neatly. He opens his desk drawer and pulls out two envelopes—the same ones he had brought to the house. He scans them, selects the one Dami had addressed to Justin Awori, and pushes it across the desk.

He chides gently. "Next time, remember your name."

Dear Justin,

I am sorry.

I missed your life. There's no excuse for a man wilfully missing his child's life.

Thankfully though, I hear you have a real father, and he's a much better man than I am. By now, I expect you understand that fatherhood is never only about blood. So, be your father's son. Be a good one. Don't be me. Enjoy your life. See-read-dance-travel the world, but never carry me as emotional baggage. You should know by now that I'm not worth it.

I will be gone by the time you read this. If I'm in the good place in the afterlife, I hope to see you someday, and hopefully, you'll let me buy you a drink, and we'll toast to your successes in spite of me.

Take care.

Dami

"Desperado"*

You skip hello. Go straight to the point. "Don't marry Henry."

She recognises your voice immediately but, catch in her throat, asks, "Kwashi?"

You think it's a good sign that she still calls you Kwashi. She usually called your full name, Tukwashi, when she was upset with you, which was plenty. "Yeah, it's me," you say.

You hear her exhale and whisper, "Shit." Knowing her, it could mean, *Oh shit, why do I have to put up with this man again?* or, *Oh shit, my feelings aren't dead yet.* You hope it's the latter.

"It's past midnight. You woke me. What do you want?"

"I told you. Don't marry Henry."

"Wait! Are you drunk again?"

"Are you changing the topic again?"

You can almost see her smile. "What do you think you're doing?"

"I'm trying to stop you from marrying Henry. Pay attention."

"Now I know you're drunk. And I can hear loud music in the background. You're probably in a club, aren't you?"

---

* Written under the influence of "Desperado" by Eagles

"No, I'm not in the club. I'm in the club's car park. You say I'm drunk. I say I'm mellow. Let's agree to disagree. And let's focus on the point of this call."

She sighs. "Why are you doing this?"

"Because I have a phone. And because I can." You try to supress a giggle, but a burp escapes.

"Seriously, why?"

"Because I need to do this. You know I'm still in love with you."

She snorts. "Nothing has hurt me as much as your so-called love. Just so you know, right now, your love is perfectly useless."

"Touché. Okay, how about your love? It should be good for something. You still love me. I know that."

"Stop."

You close your eyes and exhale. "Arese, please give me some time to get my shit together. And I'll be back. A new man. And we'll get married."

"We were married before. It didn't work out. Remember?"

"Remember what they say about trying again and again after you fail the first time? Let's prove that we're not quitters."

She chuckles. "The wedding is next week."

"I know. Just heard today."

"Chi Gal told you?"

"Yeah."

After your marriage crashed and burned, one of the few things salvaged from the wreckage was Arese's friendship with Chigala, your younger sister, whom everyone called Chi Gal. It was fascinating because they'd met once, at your wedding, and they didn't talk regularly, but when they did, the conversations were long, deep, and frighteningly honest. You encouraged it because you understood that they both had very few female friends, and you realised you were lucky that the two closest women in your life shared a fierce love for each other. When the marriage got rocky, Chi Gal played mediator, and you remember the ridiculousness once when you and Arese were in the same house in London but weren't speaking, and Chi Gal, furiously WhatsApping both of you from Port Harcourt and dispensing advice, managed to gain a temporary rapprochement.

"I see. So, tell me—how did you think this is going to end? You drunk-call me, sweet-talk me into cancelling my wedding, we get back together, live happily ever after? Is that it?"

You shrug. "Yeah, basically. But you missed the part where we adopt two kids and a dog."

Long pause. A soft, "Three." Then a sigh that cut deep like Jesus's one to Judas after the kiss. "I wanted three kids with you. Two girls and a boy. Had their names all picked out."

"We can have four now if you want."

"Must you joke about everything?"

"Yes." The word slips from your lips. You wince at yourself. "Sorry," you say.

"Well then, here's a joke for you: We're never getting back together. And I'm getting married to Henry. Laugh till you choke on that."

"Say something actually funny, and I'd laugh. Want to try again?"

"Touché." There's a smile in her voice. "Are you sure you're drunk?"

"You know me. I'm at my best when I'm drunk."

"And your worst too." She sighs. "But you're still a drunk."

You sigh. But you don't tell her that you'd been sober for nine months since you moved back to Port Harcourt—your longest stretch since you could remember—till today when you heard she was getting remarried. Instead, you say, "I will get my shit together. I promise."

"You broke every important promise . . ."

This truth breaks your heart, and for the first time that night, you have nothing to say.

"You say you love me, right? If you really love me, promise you'll do this one thing for me."

"Anything." It comes out slurred, heavy, because there's a lump in your throat.

"Leave me alone."

It was almost the same way she said it the last night you were together in London. You hope she remembers that night. That night, you'd gone back to the house and begged her to take you back, and she refused and told you to leave her alone. But she pulled you into her arms. You noticed the tears in her eyes during the lovemaking, and it threw you so hard that you stopped till she rolled her hips under you and urged you on. After, you clung to each other like it was life itself while she sobbed into your shoulders, and you stroked her thick hair.

Her divorce petition came in the post the next morning. The forms said the two grounds for divorce were your unreasonable behaviour and adultery. In her Unreasonable Behaviour Statement, she gave detailed instances of your drinking and drugtaking and added that she had corroborating videos. She also listed specifics of your affairs and one-night stands in the Adultery Statement, including the big scandal—you noticed that it was only for the last six months, but it was an embarrassingly long list—and seeing everything in black and white sucked the air and fight out of you. You'd read up about your shit before when the tabloids carried some easily denied gossip and when the big scandal of you and the three girls in the hotel room broke and wrecked your life, but it was a different read this time—cold and terrible like the opening of your life's book on Judgment Day.

You considered contesting the divorce. Her Adultery Statement was ninety-five percent correct, and you mused about being the asshole who set that five percent error on the public record straight. Plus, she didn't know you knew she'd also started sleeping with Henry (yes, you also knew it was your fault, but it was a teeny bit galling that she was pointing at your adultery while hiding hers). What stopped you was the realisation that your contest meant going through the circus of a court hearing, and none of you needed that. So, to make everything easy, you didn't contest it.

The temporary divorce order, the decree nisi, also came easy, in the post while you were away for two weeks at a private rehab place in Surrey. You read it on the day you returned, there at the doorway, your bag still slung across your shoulder. You dropped your bag, turned around, walked to your local pub, and drank yourself to oblivion. The final order came the day before you packed up and returned to Port Harcourt, right in the middle of your thirteenth attempt at rehab. You saw the envelope marked with the court's logo, but wary and wiser, you didn't open it till you were in the air. For a reason you were yet to understand, you couldn't drink while airborne. Maybe it was because you were scared shitless of flying.

You returned to Port Harcourt with a throat so parched, you'd have traded your liver for a drink. But somehow, you didn't drink. It was part miracle, part luck. Luck because you stayed with Majikpo, your elder brother and a teetotaller, for the first few weeks of your return, and there was no alcohol in his house. Luck because, as you'd been away for eighteen years, you no longer had a drinking posse like in the old days when you started out as a DJ, just your day-one paddyman, Ochuko, and he was off alcohol and on a diet because of his blood pressure. Luck because there was work. During your time in London, you'd teamed up with Ochuko to acquire a radio station, One FM, in Port Harcourt. It was one of your smarter life decisions, your retirement plan, because you never intended to grow old or die in the UK, most likely in a care home. (Though you had British citizenship having been born in London—a surprise preemie during the year your father studied for his master's and your pregnant mother came to visit him—you were raised in Port Harcourt, which, for all its shittiness, you considered your home.) You threw yourself into working at One FM, co-hosting the *Breakfast Show*, and returning every weeknight from seven to eleven p.m., premium drinking time. It saved you, and you wondered why you hadn't thought of it before. (When you'd worked in radio in London, you'd always been on the morning shows, which meant evenings were free for drinking.) Luck because Ochuko dragged you out on weekends to run and exercise.

Your luck held for nine months. Then, today, you heard she was getting remarried, and everything crashed, hard and destructive like a hurricane making landfall.

She repeats herself, this time sigh-pleading, "Leave me alone."

You hear a soft beep, and the line goes dead.

You leave her alone—until . . .

You say hello this time. "Hey."

"Hey."

It takes awhile before you speak. "I just heard."

"Who told you? Chi Gal?" Her voice is subdued, beaten.

"Yeah."

And because you never knew what to say to grieving people, all you can mumble is, "I'm sorry about your baby."

She exhales. Whispers, "Daniel. His name was Daniel."

"I'm sorry about Daniel," you say.

Six months after her wedding, and after carrying him to term, Daniel was delivered stillborn. She'd told Chi Gal the day it happened while she was still in the hospital, and they'd been on the phone almost every day since then. Chi Gal had waited two weeks before mentioning it in passing to you.

Long, awkward silence. You could have said goodbye and ended the call at that point. But because you knew her better than most people, because you knew the demons who permanently stirred that pot in her head, you say as soft as you can, "It's not your fault, you know?"

You hear her sobs over the line—clean, clear, and familiar like rain. You can't see her, but you know she's hunched, left arm folded across her midriff, head buried in her right palm, shoulders trembling. You know this because you made and watched her cry so much. You became the world's foremost expert in the subject of her misery. In the old days when she cried, you'd hold her, lie to her that you wouldn't do a particular crazy shit again, and lie to her that everything was going to be alright in the end.

You can't hold her today, but you can still talk. So, you talk. You slide into word-dropping mode, and as always when you're in that mode, your words flow smooth, soothing, and as persuasive as a roomful of conmen. As always, you don't remember the exact things you say, just the general points: that it wasn't her fault that she had sudden preeclampsia (Chi Gal had explained what it was), which was fatal to Daniel, that she and Henry should take as much time and space as they needed to grieve, that in the process of grieving, they shouldn't forget to shag because grief-shagging was criminally underrated, that you hoped they'd have kids someday though it may not stop this pain, but that was okay because no one was guaranteed anything in this life, that you always thought she'd be an excellent mother, and as much as you disliked Henry, you'd admit, grudgingly, that he was a solid, stable, perhaps dull man who won't be too shabby as a father. And in the middle of it, something profound hits you—for the first time, you're dropping words without telling a single lie. You're not sure how that makes you feel.

Like in the old days, you talk till her tears stop, and she even laughs at your stupid jokes. It crosses your mind that this was the point where, if you were still together, you'd have had crazy, feverish, make-up sex. You sigh-smile at the memories, but somehow, you know for certain at that moment that you'll never be with her again. You feel a sudden hollowness, a sense of loss, but you're surprised at how little it actually hurts you.

Maybe you're finally over her. Or maybe it's because there's a woman beside you in your bed. She's naked under the covers, and she snores softly. She's young, twenty-six, and has a fiancé. Your regular joke is that you're old enough to be her sugar daddy, but she refuses to take any money from you because something-something about fighting the patriarchy. What you have with her is hard to define, so neither of you bother with definitions. The arrangement seems to work—there are no obligations, no expectations of fidelity, no demands; the sex is enthusiastic, regular, but soulless; the conversations are okay, though her idealism and naivete make them easily tiring (but you know life will teach her soon enough). Lately, she'd talked about considering becoming vegan, and she was already so insufferably sanctimonious about it that you made a mental note to end things if she did because you didn't need that kind of negative energy in your life.

"Thank you for talking to me like this." Arese exhales. "I didn't expect this from you."

You want to reply that this wasn't a big deal, that it was the decent thing to do, and that you weren't as big a monster as she thought you were. Instead, you shrug, reach across to the glass of Guinness and palm wine by your bedside, and sip.

Maybe she heard you, or maybe it was an eerie coincidence, but she asks, "Do you still drink?"

You chuckle. "Only one day at a time."

You're drinking sour brandy, preparing for your seven to eleven p.m. weekday show, when she calls. You see her name on your phone's caller ID, and before you answer, you refill your snifter.

"Hey."

"Hey."

"Surprised I called?"

Sip. "Not anymore."

"How've you been?"

"So-so. You?"

"Fine."

Pause.

"How's working on Nigerian radio been?"

Sip. "Same as British radio, I guess. I entertain some people, piss off others, but get all of them to keep listening."

"That's good."

"I hear you've gone back to DJing too."

"More producing songs than DJing, actually."

"That's good."

Pause. "I want to talk to you about something."

There's a familiar kick in your chest because whenever she said these words during your marriage, you were in trouble. Like in the old days, you respond, impulsively, by making silly jokes. "If you're about to tell me that you want to leave Henry, and you're about to beg me to take you back, the answer is no."

"What!"

"Sister, I said what I said." You hide your chuckle in a sip.

"Oh! I hear you're dating some lawyer. Is it because of her you won't take me back?"

"Chi Gal talks too much."

"Tell me about her."

"Who? ID?"

"Is that her name?"

"Yes. Short form. Full name is Idara."

"What's she like?"

You pause, smile. "She's fire: fascinating, warm, dangerous."

"Wow."

"Technically, we've not started dating."

"Why? You're usually quick with these things."

You hesitate. "I think she's a great one. So, I'm taking my time. Don't want to mess up."

"I see. So, because of her, you won't take me back."

You sigh. "I was just joking about all that."

"I know. I was just messing with you." And you can tell she's smiling her crinkled-eyed, one-dimpled-cheek smile.

So, you smile. "Still won't take you back though."

"Never thought of coming back." She corrects herself. "What I meant to say is, I won't come back though."

"I know." Sip. "So, what about an occasional shag for old times' sake? You know I'll make the perfect side piece."

"Tukwashi!"

But she's laughing. You remember how you used to make her laugh till tears stood in her eyes, and after she'd look at you like you'd gifted her something precious. And that's the moment you know—a part of you will always love Arese, but finally, you're over her. You wait for her to finish laughing, then you ask, "You wanted to speak to me about something?"

"Yes. This is likely to be a hard conversation, but I'll just go ahead with it."

You sense that this conversation is about to floor you. You bottom-up your glass, courage to face the incoming wave.

"You didn't tell me you were raped as a child."

It takes some time before you respond. Then you say, "Chi Gal talks too much."

"She thought I knew."

"It wasn't rape-rape. Like there was no force and . . ." You stop yourself and sigh. "She was the house-help who stayed with us for many years. . . . She was older. . . . I was . . . Do you know how many guys whose house-helps did . . . who had their first experience with house-helps? It was common. . . . Not a big deal . . . Chi Gal shouldn't have . . ."

"She was shocked as I was when she found out."

Mercy worked for your family from when Chi Gal was a toddler and you were in primary school till sometime in the middle of your senior secondary school (SS1 or SS2, you can't remember exactly when). You didn't know where she moved on to, and you didn't care. She didn't cross your mind for years till last week when you hung out with Chi Gal and she mentioned that they'd reconnected recently. According to Chi Gal, Mercy, now in her fifties, looked eighty because of how viciously life had chewed her up and spat her out. In the middle of you and Chi Gal making plans to send Mercy some money and reminiscing about your childhood, you'd let it slip. That was the first time you'd mentioned it to anyone. Chi Gal pressed you for details, and you'd clammed shut and changed the topic.

"Have you talked to anyone about it?"

"Hell no! Never." Your tone is little too forceful for your liking.

"I thought as much."

You speak slowly. "It's not a big deal."

"If you say so. But for me, it explains a lot about you."

You roll your eyes and sigh. "Abegi."

"When we met, you told me a few things. Your parents' fighting and eventual divorce, your early days DJing. I suspect this fills in many of the gaps."

"What gaps?"

"Like why you drink to forget, and why you—"

"What?"

"Aye. You're a morose drinker. You hide in it, just like you hide in music and in your jokes. And I never quite understood what you were hiding from."

"For once, can you stop trying to psychoanalyse me?"

You'd met Arese in your early days on British radio. You were the junior co-host of a morning show, and she'd come in as a guest to talk about mental health and suicide rates on behalf of the charity she worked for. The attraction was instant, and you could tell it was mutual because she let you catch her stealing glances at you, and she laughed a little too hard at your jokes. Then, in the middle of talking about depression, she made a point about people who hide theirs behind humour while looking hard at you. That was the first time she psychoanalysed you. Later, you got her number from the radio station's researcher, and she recognised your voice when you said hello but hadn't identified yourself, and she chuckled and said, "I knew you'd call."

Extraordinary sex on the first date, and with that out of the way, you got down to the business of knowing each other. You took her along to your DJing gigs, which you were doing as a side hustle, and taught her how to dance; she took you to the homeless shelters and soup kitchens where she volunteered. She taught you Geordie accent and slang because she was born and raised in Newcastle. You taught her pidgin because she was trying to discover her Nigerian roots (her Nigerian father died when she was five, and she was raised by her English mother). She lived in Gospel Oak at the time, so your dates were usually picnics at the grassy fields and rolling hills of the nearby Hampstead Heath. It was summer, the days were so long that the sun pretended it would never set, and one evening, with the grass tickling your feet and the sky achingly beautiful because God was showing off, and you were feeling the closest you've ever been to peace, she closed the book she'd been reading, lifted her head from your chest, and said, "When you're ready, you'll admit you're in love with me." And you smiled, closed your eyes, but you don't tell her that it was your first time in love, and you had no idea what to do.

"I decided to talk to you about this because I think you need help, to sort yourself out before you go into another relationship and wreck another woman. And because the way you talked to me helped me deal with losing Daniel. So, this is me returning the favour by talking to you with the hope that it helps you get on your way to start dealing with this."

You snap. "Thank you. Now we're even."

"That's not what I meant."

You sigh. "I'm on-air soon. I've got to go." You end the call.

You skip hello. Go straight to the point. "I was seven when she started."

For a moment, you don't hear anything. You wonder if the call had gone off, but you look at your phone and see it's still on. Then you wonder if the alcohol had deadened your sense—you'd been drinking absinthe neat because you wanted the fastest route to drunken bliss (but you were getting frustrated because it was giving you a strange kind of lucidity instead). That's when you hear her heavy breathing.

You continue talking, but your words trip over themselves as they tumble out.

"The first time . . . I remember . . . she was naked apart from her blouse. . . . She made me . . . she made me . . . I remember tasting a bit of her urine . . . Another time, it was the remnant of what I later found out was menstrual blood . . ." You chuckle. "So yeah, when you and I were together, and you said I had a magic tongue . . . these are some of the things I had to experience so I could learn the magic."

"Don't joke about this," she whispers.

You chug straight from the bottle. "Oh, there's another funny one. The first time I came. I was eleven. I didn't know what the shit was. Before that day, I was . . . used to shagging . . . and being stroked but . . . there was no . . . happy ending . . . and I couldn't understand it in my head, and I think I got . . . frustrated because I could sense something was missing. So that day, as usual, she puts her hand in my shorts and touches me, but suddenly, boom, sweet sticky icky . . . I swear, it felt like I'd moved to heaven and all my Christmases came through at once. I had to have that feeling again.

Fucked my head up because there I was, a little bastard, walking around with a permanent pencil-stub hard-on, mentally undressing every woman I saw, an animal, always in heat. In addition to all we were doing, I was masturbating so much I must have been shedding skin every week."

"This is not funny."

"If I don't laugh, I'll cry."

"When did it stop?"

"She left when I was fourteen."

"This explains why you've never been faithful to any woman in your life."

"Don't!"

"Don't what?"

"Don't coddle me, please. I'm a grown man. I can take responsibility for my fuckups. It wasn't Mercy who made me not have self-control. It wasn't Mercy who put me in that hotel room with those girls."

You'd met the three girls at a private party in Bristol where you'd DJ'd. Typical party girls—in their twenties, legs for days, bronze-tanned in January because sunbeds smirked at winter—looking to have a good night. After your set, they followed you back to your hotel room for the after-party. You won't remember any of their names until the next morning. You remember some dancing and drinking till you were legless. You remember doing some weed. You remember they offered you some pills, but you said no because they weren't your thing. You remember one snorting coke from another's cleavage while the third blew you as you splayed out on the couch. That's all you remembered before you passed out. When you woke, you were half-naked and had a hangover meant for Dionysus himself. But what shook you was there was an army of emergency medical personnel and policemen in your room. Long story short, one of the girls had overdosed and had just been taken away in an ambulance. Eventually, they took you and the other two down to the police station for questioning. You'd finished with the police and were about to leave when the news came through that the girl was dead. You didn't face any charges, but you lost everything in the fallout—your day job on radio, most of your DJing gigs, and of course, Arese. You couldn't blame her. Your marriage was already in trouble, but till then, your screw-ups were private, and she could bow her head in shame and bear them. This was different. You moved out of the house into a bedsit. Three weeks later, she filed for divorce.

"You know why I can't bring myself to blame Mercy fully? Because a part of me enjoyed it." You exhale. "Don't misunderstand me—at the time, I sensed it was wrong, a part of me was disgusted with her, still is, and disgusted with myself for letting it happen and liking it. But yeah, I liked it." You sigh. "Analyse that."

It takes a long time for her to speak. Then, she whispers, "You're so perfectly fucked up, it's amazing."

"I know."

She tries to talk again but sighs and sighs like her thoughts have refused to morph into words. Finally, she blurts, "Promise me you'll get help for this."

You chuckle. "Last time we spoke about promises, you reminded me that I broke every promise I made to you. Are you sure you want to go down this route?"

"You better make this promise, and you better fucking keep it." She's almost snarling.

"I hear you."

But you don't make the promise. Because life was never that simple, and life never promised anything. What you did know though was that tomorrow, or the day after, or sometime soon, you'd put down the bottle, and for the nth time attempt to wean yourself off alcohol. You also know that over the past months, you'd cut down on DJing because it involved parties, and parties led to more casual sex. Maybe it was because you were older and wiser; maybe you were tired of it all; or maybe it was because, subconsciously, you were preparing your best self for ID. And if you fell off any of these wagons, you'd climb back on again. You don't know if you'll win, but you'll keep trying. And that's the moment you know, win or lose, that someday your wandering heart will rest, and you'll be free.

You don't tell Arese any of this. You don't tell her that you're thankful for her, that you appreciated her call, three weeks ago, to talk to you about this even though you'd cut her off. You don't let her know you're pleased that somehow, against all the odds, you had both developed the unlikeliest of friendships and were now at peace with each other. You don't say that you're grateful she loved you once, and even though she'd never love you like that again, right now, she's on the other end of the line, breathing heavily and silently wishing you well—and it was a big fucking deal because it was a lot more than you deserved.

"Thank you." That's all you can say.

She doesn't reply. But you know she understands.

"You Suppose Know"*

I was intrigued by Mr. and Mrs. Ngofa before I met them.

Tonse, one of my bosses and a co-owner of the hospital where I worked as a physician and cardiologist, called me on the intercom one day. "My parents are coming over this morning. My dad's not feeling well, and my mum has finally convinced him to see a doctor. That itself is a miracle. I want you to see him. You know I can't do it."

There was a rule: in the hospital, doctors didn't attend to their families. Besides, Tonse was an OB-GYN.

I asked, "Ikenna is aware?" Ikenna was one of Tonse's partners and the head of general medicine. I reported to him.

"I spoke to Ikenna. He recommended you."

So, I said, "Sure."

"Thanks. Also, let me know if anything is wrong with him, okay?"

"Yes, sir."

---

* Written under the influence of "You Suppose Know" (Remix) by Bez ft. Yemi Alade

"One more thing. My parents can be . . . ," he hesitated, "a handful."

"How? What do you mean?"

He laughed. "You'll see. Have fun." He hung up.

Two hours later, a nurse knocked on the door of the consulting room and came in with a file for my next patient. I did a quick scan. First visit to the hospital. Name: Osaro Ngofa. Age: seventy-five. Height: an even six feet. Overweight but not yet obese. Blood pressure was a little high but nothing too unusual. I asked the nurse to show him in.

As expected, he entered with his wife by his side. She was buxomly, almost as tall as he was, and greyed out gracefully like him. I stood as they walked in, smiled, and introduced myself. After settling them in the chairs in front of the desk, I asked, "So how can I help you?"

She spoke. "We're here because of my husband, Professor Ngofa."

"Mister," he corrected. To me, he said, "Mr. Ngofa is fine, thank you."

"Nonsense. Professor is a valid title, not like those attention-seeking ones like engineer or surveyor." Her voice was a song; her words flowed smoothly into themselves, rhythmic, rising, falling, soothing. His was deep, authoritative.

"Mister."

"Professor."

They turned to me like they expected me to cast a deciding vote on what to call him. I voted wisely. "Okay, sir. How can I help you?"

I could have sworn their eyes were smiling.

"He's not feeling well."

"I am well, Nimi." He sighed at her. He turned to me. "It's nothing really."

"How exactly are you feeling, sir. Any pain?"

"No pain. He's weak, fatigued. He's been eating more but has lost some weight."

"Nimi."

She ignored him. "He has also been going to the bathroom more."

"No, I haven't."

"Usually, it was once or twice a night. Now, it's four to six times on average. On Wednesday last week, he went seven times."

"I have been drinking a lot more water lately; that's why."

"You're not the expert here, darling. She is. Let her examine you and decide if it's just water." She turned to me. "My dear, I have to monitor these things, or else, he won't notice them. It's the burden some of us wives have to bear. Are you married, dear? I didn't notice a ring."

"Yes, ma'am. I don't wear my ring at work. Nature of the job."

"Then I'm sure you understand. You know how husbands can be sometimes."

I quickly asked them about the basics of his health history. No smoking. A beer every other day. At least three coffees every day. No exercise ("though he's a member of the Golf Club," she added with a cheeky smile). No history of heart or other illnesses, apart from the occasional malaria. I examined him, his heart, lungs (in the past year, I'd taken more care with respiratory examinations due to the soot pollution in Port Harcourt). I checked his eyes, asked if his vision was sometimes blurry lately. It had. As I examined him, he said with what seemed to be pride, "I'm in perfect health. The last time I was in a hospital was thirty-five years ago when my daughter was born."

"He's also afraid of hospitals," she quipped.

"No, I'm not."

I turned away to hide my smile. His heart was racing when I examined him. After I was done with the physical examination, I started filling in my notes and said, "We need to run some tests."

"What tests?"

"Blood tests for now, sir." I gave what I hoped was a reassuring smile. "In the room down the corridor, they'll draw some blood from you for the tests and take it down to the lab. The results should be out in an hour. Then I'll see you again to brief you. You can wait, or you can come back—"

"I want you to draw the blood," he said hesitantly. She nodded her agreement. "You can do that, right?" That was the first time I realised that behind the bickering, they were really a close team.

I nodded. "Yes, I can."

"So, you'll do it, right?"

I smiled. "It'll be my pleasure, sir."

His eyes crinkled as he beamed. White teeth. "Good. Because we like you. We're comfortable with you," she explained.

And I understood then that he was also afraid of needles.

So, as I prepared for the venepuncture, I got him to talk. He told me about his three children—Tonse, Kenwi, and Ngo—as I tied the tourniquet on the upper part of his arm and asked him to make a fist so I could find a vein. He was talking about his six grandkids when I slipped the needle in. He winced, I nodded like I was more interested in his story, and he continued. He was in the middle of a funny tale of how Tonse's last child, a toddler, kept trying to drink his beer when I filled and labelled the tubes and finished.

They said they preferred to wait for the result, so I ushered them to a private waiting room. I asked if they wanted to see Tonse, and they said no because they understood he was busy at the time. I got them some water and left. I attended to three patients before his results came through.

I studied the results for a long time. Then I took the file to Ikenna, and we talked about it. He agreed with me. Afterwards, I walked to the other wing of the hospital to look for Tonse. Luckily, I found him at a watercooler on a break from his patients. I gave him the results. He was deadpan as he studied them. When he finished, all he said was, "Do what you have to do."

I returned to the consulting room, and I called them back in. I waited for them to get comfortable, and then I spoke softly. "I'm afraid the news is not too good. You appear to have type 2 diabetes. It should be manageable long-term. However, short-term, from the results, your blood sugar reading is sky high. We have to admit you in the hospital at once."

"I've not entered a hospital for thirty-five years. I'm not starting now. I feel fine."

"Sir, I hear what you're saying. However, the numbers in your blood work are such that no doctor will think it's safe for you to walk out now. You're at risk of going into a diabetic coma. What I suggest is that you stay here, just for a few days while we monitor you and give you medication to bring down your blood sugar. When it's down to comfortable levels, you can return home, and we'll advise you on long-term care to monitor your blood sugar, if you require insulin, lifestyle, and dietary changes—things like that."

He shook his head, but she overruled him by asking me, "I presume there's a private room in this hospital?"

"Yes, ma'am."

"With two beds?"

"Two beds?"

"Yes. I will be here with him. And hospital beds are notoriously small." She raised an eyebrow. "Who do you expect will take care of my husband while he's here?"

I wanted to mention that we had nurses, and the hospital's rules forbade family members staying overnight with patients, but instead I said, "We'll have the two beds in the room, ma'am."

Just before I closed that night, I went with Tonse to check on his father.

We found his parents cuddled, lying on the same bed, ignoring the second bed that had been wheeled into the room. They smiled when we walked in but didn't break their hold.

Tonse smirked. "I thought you people wanted two beds."

Mr. Ngofa said, "As you can see, she's always in my space."

She raised her head slightly to glare at him. "I'm here because I'm nursing you."

He snorted. "Ha! You're marking your territory in the guise of nursing me. Isn't this a hospital? Aren't there nurses here?"

"Some pretty ones too," Tonse added. He winked at his father. "Just say the word, and I'll send them your way."

She turned to her husband. "You think they can put up with you?"

"Let's give them a chance to try and see."

She sighed. "Ungrateful man. As for you, Tonse, you're no longer my son. I disown you."

"This is the fifth time you've disowned me this month, Ma." He leaned down and kissed her cheek.

"Foolish boy."

"I love you too, Ma."

She snuggled into her husband, and he held her tighter.

Tonse made a sour face. "You people should get a room abeg."

Mrs. Ngofa retorted, "We already got a room. And you're in it."

"My apologies. I'll leave soon."

"Please do."

"Whatever you do, sha, don't break our bed. Hospital policy is break and pay. Don't think you're exempt because you're my family."

I managed to pause the back and forth to confirm that he'd taken his medication. I asked if he was comfortable. He was. I asked if he had eaten. He had—Kokoma, Tonse's wife, had brought food for them after calling me to confirm the new dietary rules.

Then, they flipped it on me. They asked how my day was. Fine. How I was. I said fine again. He said I looked tired. She said I looked dead on my feet. I smiled because they were right. They asked if I'd eaten. No. The last time I ate? Breakfast, I admitted. She tutted at Tonse, disapproval for "overworking" me. He laughed and lied that he'd do something about it. They thanked me and again said how much they liked me. They also told Tonse, jokingly, to increase my salary. He promised to look into it, another lie. They asked for my mobile number because, as they'd said before, they were comfortable with me. I gave it to them.

As I left the room with Tonse, I asked, "Have they always been like this?"

He grinned. "As far as I can remember, yes."

I blew out my cheeks. "They're interesting."

"Brace yourself. They're going to adopt you tomorrow."

He was right. Kind of.

The next day, they sent me lunch—jollof, chicken, and a salad—in takeaway packs. I called Tonse to ask him the best way I could politely decline. He laughed and told me not to be silly. That's how it started. They sent food to me every day for the period he was in the hospital. They asked that I spend my breaks with them to chill, eat, talk. The times I spent with them were short, but they became the highlight of my working day. They were curious about me but not nosy about it. Their constant bantering made me smile. On the night before I discharged him, I asked how they met.

They told the story together.

"1971. After the war. I followed my friend, Osita, to court. He's Igbo and was suing to recover his house in Port Harcourt that someone had taken over after he fled the city during the Biafra War. We were waiting for his case to be called when I saw her—the only female lawyer in the courtroom. And she was cross-examining her husband."

"Wait. What?"

"She was representing herself in her own divorce. So, yes, she was asking him questions."

She shrugged. "I was a young lawyer, just starting out. I couldn't afford to pay another lawyer. So, I did it myself. I wouldn't recommend it for anybody though."

"She was polite and calm and methodical, but she knew how to bait him. She bloodied him in that witness box, and at some point, everyone could see he was lying. She was magnificent, and I had to see her again." He shook his head, a faraway smile on his face as he remembered.

"So, he stalked me."

"Her case was adjourned. I noted the date it was adjourned to, and I came to court on that day. I followed the case till the end."

"Then, he behaved like a schoolboy."

"I passed her a note in court. Immediately after the judge made the provisional order of divorce."

"What did the note say?"

He chuckled. "That I wanted to hire her as my lawyer."

"He started off by lying to me."

"Of course, I didn't want to hire her, but as her case had ended and I didn't know how to see her again, it was the only thing I could think of. Eventually, I told her the truth."

"After leading me on for two weeks."

"At first, she said she wasn't interested. She did shakara for a long time. Nine months, I think."

"I don't know what he expected. The ink from my divorce wasn't even dry yet."

"Eventually, we got together. And we decided to get married. But everybody opposed it."

"Why?"

"He's Eleme; I'm Okrika. Our tribes are neighbours, but they've fought on and off for years. It was a lot worse at that time. My parents found out about him in the middle of one of those intermittent wars. Plus, my ex-husband's people, Okrikans too, were still bitter about the divorce."

"My folks talked about the Okrika-Eleme thing too. And they didn't want me marrying a divorcee, especially so soon after the divorce."

"And it wasn't so soon. We're talking two years after."

I asked, "So you finally convinced them?"

They laughed. She said, "No. We went to the registry one day and got married. Only our mothers came."

"It was such a scandal in those days."

"We all finally made peace when Tonse was born."

I hesitated. "Your ex-husband?"

"I knew him from when we were little. My family and his were close. They moved to Lagos a year before the war. During the war, we were evacuated from Port Harcourt and stayed in their house in Lagos. I managed to get called to the Bar. We were just two Okrika children in a strange land, and we stood no chance. Our parents match-made us."

"Why did you get divorced?"

A cloud crossed her face for a moment. "He raped a woman. His secretary. Of course, he denied it when she told me, but I knew he did it."

"How?"

"He used to rape me." She smiled stiffly. "Technically, under Nigerian law, a man can't rape his wife. But Nigerian law didn't live in the same house with Miebaka. So, since I couldn't get him charged for rape, I did the only thing I could. I got a divorce."

She saw the look on my face. "My dear, don't feel sorry for me. It was such a long time ago."

"I'm . . ." I processed my thoughts before I continued. "I'm dismayed that he walked away scot free."

"I never said he did." A smile played by the corners of her mouth, but she didn't let it out. "Sometime after the divorce, some unknown young men, of the rougher sort, accosted him one night outside the bar he frequented. They beat him to within an inch of his life. Broke some teeth and two fingers. I heard that he never knew why they attacked him."

Finally, she half smiled. "Sometimes, I wish they'd told him why."

They were back in the hospital about three months later.

I'd been following up with phone calls, and she told me it wasn't going well. Eventually, she dragged him again to the hospital. I ran new tests. His blood sugar was not as high as the first time I saw him, but it was worrying.

She said, "He sneaks out to eat all the things that are bad for him. He's not following the diet plan."

"Because the diet plan has too many abominations. Brown basmati rice, wheat bread, boiled unripe plantains. Even your soups and stews taste watered down. If they were coffee, they'd be weak decaf." He shook his head.

Her eyes flashed. "What are you trying to say about my cooking?"

It wasn't banter. There was an undercurrent of tetchiness, and I realised they'd been fighting a lot. I turned peacemaker. "Dietary changes can be hard, but I'm sure we can work out something. Maybe review a few things in the diet." I focused on him. "Meanwhile, I hope you're doing some moderate exercise as we discussed."

She snorted. "Ha!"

His grin was guilty and silly and endearing all at once.

It made me crack a smile even though I didn't want to. I said, "I'm going to place you on insulin. I'll explain in a minute." I turned and began filling his file.

Later that evening after they'd gone, Tonse knocked on the door of my consulting room and popped his head in. "My mother told me what happened today."

I shrugged.

"Insulin, eh?"

"Yes. It had to be done."

"I know." He walked in and slouched in the patient's chair. "I doubt he'll take it consistently."

"I've advised him of the possible implications if he doesn't."

He sighed. "I know."

"I don't understand. Why is he like that?"

"He doesn't really mean to. He's forgetful, absentminded. Then, he doesn't like people telling him what to do; so, subconsciously, he fights too many unnecessary battles. A bad combination."

"Can't your mother talk to him?"

"She always does. You've seen them na. But when you've been married to someone for forty-four years, no matter how much you love them, you learn how to tune them out sometimes."

"Can't you talk to him?"

He shook his head. "My father's a gentleman's gentleman. But he's also the most obstinate man I know." A faraway look came in his eye. "I remember when I was young. He was an active member of ASUU, the lecturers' union, and he was a vocal critic of the government. This was back in the military days. I used to eavesdrop on her telling him to tone it down because of his family. The man carried on because he believed in whatever it was he believed in. In '88, ASUU went on one of their usual strikes, and the military regime proscribed them. My father still refused to hear word. They arrested him. Detained him in Enugu for about a month. She'd drive to Enugu from Port Harcourt three or four times a week to send him food. She filed lawsuits, spoke to people on his behalf. Eventually, they released him. Did he hear word after he was released? No. In 1990, he and his ASUU guys attend a conference, and in the middle of their anti-military gra-gra, the Orkar coup happens. After foiling the coup, the government was happy to use the opportunity to link some of its enemies to it. He was locked up for two months this time. Somehow, she got him off, again. He was lucky. The guys he was arrested with weren't so lucky. They faced a military tribunal."

He sighed. "So yeah, as inseparable as they are, if his wife can't convince him about a thing, nobody else can."

The call came on my day off. It was late in the morning, and I was still in bed spooning Kaniye, my husband. My phone rang. It was Amanda from the hospital's front desk. She said, "Sorry to bother you today, Deola."

"Hey, Amanda. What's up?"

"They just brought in one of your patients. They're in Casualty. It looks serious."

"Which patient?"

"Ngofa."

"My God."

"You don't need to come. Dr. Ikenna and a team are already on it. I figured you'd want to know."

"You figured right, Amanda. Thank you."

I shook Kaniye's shoulder. "You need to take me to the hospital now, please. I'm not in the best mood to drive." As I spoke, I was already on my feet, praying in my mind, rummaging through the wardrobe for what to wear.

He was used to me like that. He rolled off the bed, tapped my buttocks, and said, "I guess you're not taking a shower."

"I don't have the time."

He smiled and kissed me. "Brush sha. You have morning breath."

"Thank God you're here, Deola," Ikenna boomed. His voice was gruff and unnaturally loud, like an agbero god.

It was organised chaos in the Resus. Ikenna had summoned a full team, including the radiographer and respiratory therapist. They surrounded the bed, some darted back and forth, and they worked as quickly and calmly as they could. A screen covered the bed from view, but I managed to catch a glimpse of the familiar grey hair of the person on it. I had been in the Resus enough to be able to gauge the hopes and mood of any working team—and this was sombre.

"What do you want me to do? Should I go change and join the team?"

"No. For this one, I'm treating you like you're the patient's family. Just like him." He pointed at Tonse, who was at a corner frowning and pacing. "I want you to take him out of here and keep him out so I can do my work. He's refusing to listen to me."

As I walked to Tonse, he scowled at me. "Don't talk me out of this, Deola."

I gave a half shrug. "You know Ikenna is right. Neither of us should be here. If shoes were flipped, you'd do the same."

He shook his head.

I opened my arms. "They say we're family now." I wrapped my arms around him, felt his heart beat his fear as I held him. "Let's go, bro."

Ikenna had knock knees. I'd worked with him for six years but noticed his k-leg for the first time that day when he came out of the Resus and walked towards us.

We stood.

From Ikenna's face, I already knew. He stopped in front of Tonse, reached up, and put both hands on his shoulder. Even at that moment, they were incongruous together—one stocky, the other strapping.

"I'm sorry, bro. We did all we could." Ikenna said this as softly as he could manage.

Tonse nodded slowly and managed to keep his professional mask on. "What happened?"

"Right now, it looks like a ruptured brain aneurysm."

I shook my head. With them, there are usually no warning signs.

Tonse nodded again, wiped the tears that suddenly stood in his eyes, and sniffed. He extricated himself from Ikenna. "Thanks, man."

He sad smiled, hugged me, and said, "Sis." When we broke, he wiped his eyes with the back of his palm and said, "My father has been waiting in my office for news. I'm going to break his heart when I tell him that the love of his life just died."

"We should play less chess and make love more."

He smiled. "Those were my last words to her. And she laughed. I'm happy the last thing I did for her was to make her laugh." He'd told me about his last words to her many times. I didn't mind hearing it again and again.

He sat up in their bed, on what used to be her side of the bed, propped, and surrounded by pillows of different shapes and sizes. He'd told me he never used to have time for the pillows. They were hers, and they used to argue about why she needed so many for their bed. Now, before he could sleep, he'd spritz the pillows with Shalimar by Guerlain, her signature perfume, and bury himself in them. His children had bought several bottles of the perfume so he wouldn't run out. The bedroom, the house, reeked of the stuff.

It was four months after the funeral. He had lost weight and was sicker more frequently. But he refused to come to the hospital. We understood. The last time he was there, his wife died. His children got a full-time nurse to live with him to check his blood sugar and ensure he took his medication and insulin. But he either ignored her or refused to cooperate. So, I came in almost every day. It was difficult, but I became the only person who could convince him, albeit not every time, to eat and take his medication regularly.

We played chess too. He beat me every time, and every time, he'd remind me that on average, his wife beat him eight out of every ten times they played. His games with Kaniye were more evenly matched. One Sunday after church, Kaniye had brought me to his house, and they met and took to each other. So now, sometimes, Kaniye came with me to see him. Like today.

We heard the crunch of tyres on gravel as a car pulled into the drive leading to the house. We knew it was Tonse. With time and without ever talking about it, his children, their spouses, and I had developed a rolling shift to spend time with him.

Tonse came in, still in his scrubs. He hugged me, shook hands with Kaniye, plopped in bed next to his father, and said, "I brought Miss World DVDs so you can choose a girlfriend from there. I also brought suya. Do we eat now or later?"

It forced a half smile from him. "There're no DVDs, Tonse. You wouldn't dare."

"I'll surprise you one day. You'll see. So . . . suya. Now or later?"

"Later."

Eating suya with his late wife was another almost daily ritual. So, Tonse ate suya and tried to banter like his mother, Kokoma and Wobia cooked and doted on him, Ngo called every day from America where she lived, and we played chess. Everybody had a role.

Soon, it was time for Kaniye and me to leave. When we stood up and hugged him, he gave us his usual goodbye. "Be good to each other. Love your love. Life is short."

Tonse walked us outside. When we stopped in front of our car, he said softly, "You know he's going to die soon, right?"

I didn't answer.

He sighed. "All this we're doing . . . we can fill the empty house, but we can never fill the gaping hole where his heart used to be. He doesn't know how to live without her." He sighed again. "I'd be surprised if he lasts till the end of the year. My siblings and I have talked about it, and we're just . . ." His words trailed off and he shrugged. "You're family. We thought you should know so you can brace yourself." He looked at me. "But I suspect you know this already."

My tears came when we got into the car. Kaniye parked by the side of the road, undid our seatbelts, and leaned across the gear shift to hold me. He held me as the sobs wracked my body till it mellowed to gentle whimpers. His T-shirt was wet on one shoulder with my tears and snot.

"One day, one of us is going to die first."

"So?"

"I don't know how to feel about that."

He thought about it for a moment. "If it makes you feel better, we can pray that we die together. In an accident or something."

"This isn't a joke."

"Okay. But just so you know, if you die first, I'm going to watch Miss World DVDs sha."

I muffled my chuckle in his shoulder. Then I bit him. He laughed and rubbed my back. "Let's go home. To paraphrase a wise man—we should talk less about death and make love more."

The End

Author's Note

This is a story of an unforeseen detour and how music saved my writing.

My first published novel, *Tomorrow Died Yesterday*, came out in December 2010. In mid-2012, I started work on a proposed second novel. I had a title for it (a big deal because I struggle with titles), and I wrote so joyously fast that I expected to finish by the end of 2012 or by the first quarter of 2013 at the latest. I wrote till September 2012 when I went for my post-graduate studies for a year.

I haven't written another word of that novel since.

I tried many times to write. And every time, I met a blank—wall, screen, paper, and mind. I didn't write for years, and it messed with my mind. I won't go into the details, except to say that it got dark enough in my head for me to believe that *Tomorrow Died Yesterday* was a one-off, and I could no longer write fiction.

I almost accepted it as fate, mourned, turned, and started listening to music.

I've always listened to music. From childhood, I was deep braised in it, and now, it's almost as necessary in my life as breathing. But at that time, listening felt different, almost religious, a daily immersion and meditation in sounds and lyrics. And one day while listening to Erick Sermon and Marvin Gaye's "Music," I was struck by the lyric about wishing music could adopt one. That became the kernel for the story of a teenager with a troubled and unravelling family. Because I was scraping the bottom of the creativity barrel at the time, I couldn't even think up new characters. So, I had to turn to some of the characters in my now-abandoned novel and set the story, prequel-like, at a time before the novel. By happy coincidence, the narrator in the story was also an established DJ in the novel, and so, I added his struggle to play his first gig in the story. That was how I wrote the story *Music*—with "Music" and other songs playing in the background, whispering in my ear, egging me on.

When I finished, I struggled with a title till I decided, on a whim, to title it after the song that inspired it. It's not my favourite story in this collection, but it's my most important because it confirmed that I could write fiction again.

Buoyed by that knowledge, I went back to my novel.

But again, I spent months staring at it, not writing a single new word. Eventually, I took another break, listened to some more music, let the songs freestyle with and unlock the stories in my head, and then I wrote. It became a pattern: the non-writing of the novel, the taking of breaks to listen to music and exercise my creative muscles, the writing of stories partly influenced by the music, and the return to moping at the novel.

Sometime in 2017, with four stories written (three of which had been published online at the time), I decided to temporarily give up the pretence of working on the novel and focus on stories. By then, I had a formula (let lyrics or songs kickstart a story, write the story, title it after one of the songs); the formula wasn't broken, and I wasn't trying to fix it.

Nevertheless, some stories were harder to write than others, but thankfully, I've forgotten which ones now. I remember the remarkable ones though. Like when I reheard U2's "Song for Someone" and that first lyric about a face not spoiled by beauty, and simultaneously, it reminded me of the description of Christ in Isaiah 53:2 and birthed the character Ukela. And the extraordinary backstory for "In the City"—I heard the song by Brymo once, and immediately, I saw the story, clear like a vision down to the sequence and minutiae of each scene in my mind, and I wrote it almost exactly as I saw it. Crazy, inexplicable, but I'm thankful for that miracle.

So, that's the story of how I set out to write a sophomore novel but ended up with a collection of stories instead. And, though it was largely unplanned, I wouldn't have it any other way now. *God's Plan.*

Looking back at most of the stories, I'm pleased to see common themes: a broken people's search, conscious or not, for redemption, for a filling for the God-sized hole in their souls, for forgiveness (for self and from others), and a soft reminder that, as clichéd as it may sound, the things that really matter in this short life of ours are love and family (and music, of course). I'm old-fashioned, so I'm hoping that people who read the stories will discover these and other themes for themselves, and that some (who need it) may be gently nudged down paths of reconciliation and healing. If that fails, I'll settle for the hope that the stories will provide some entertainment and an interesting way to pass the time.

The stories are all set mainly in Port Harcourt. Why? Because I was raised there, and like all first loves, I carry a piece of the city in my heart wherever I am. Because the world needs more stories about Port Harcourt. And because, why not?

A final word on the music. I hope these stories make people go on to (re)discover and enjoy the songs that inspired them. And for creatives in the middle of temporary struggles with their work, I hope music, that deceptively powerful force, comes to free you.

As for me, it's time to listen to more music. Or write other stories. Or try again to finish that novel.

We'll see.

Chimeka Garricks

Acknowledgments

First, in the immortal words of ABBA, thank you for the music. Thanks to everyone—artistes, songwriters, bands, producers, etc.—behind the trove of music that raised me, saved me, and made me dance. You inspired and encouraged this.

Chikodili Emelumadu, you were invaluable in my writing of "I Put a Spell on You." Buddha wouldn't have been Buddha without you. Daalu.

Georgina Ilechie, thanks for reading and for your helpful feedback. Dilys Iyalla-Harry, my first-level editor, you're a star. Someday soon, the world will look up, see you, and be awed. The eagle-eyed Nathaniel Bivan and the Masobe Books team, thanks for your editorial help and for polishing this collection.

To my fellow travellers along this path—Zukiswa Wanner, Abubakar Adam Ibrahim, and TJ Benson—thanks for the gifts of your time and honest words. I am in your debt.

The visionary, Othuke Ominiabohs—I'm yet to meet someone as passionate about books as you. And you're damn persuasive. This world will be a better place when your dreams come true.

Kalaf Epalanga, Stefanie Hirsbrunner, Karla Colorno, and

Musa Okwonga—without knowing it, you all helped make this happen. Thank you.

Daniella Wexler, Ghjulia Romiti, and the HarperCollins team, thanks for taking a chance on this and for all your support.

Sharon Bowers, you read the stories and sent me an unforgettable email that made a grown man cry. And you fought for me. Thank you.

Ibiso Graham-Douglas, you're that friend who, according to the Bible, sticks closer than a sister. Thank you for always being in my corner.

Bisi Adjapon, our friendship is such a beautiful thing. Thanks for being a guiding light on this journey.

Biyai—right hand, light of my world, love of my life, wife—you always believed, even when I lost my faith.

Finally, God. For love, life, and the gifts. Hope I make you proud. Thank you.

A Note on the Cover

Since *A Broken People's Playlist* is a collection in which each story is inspired by a song, it was obvious that the cover, too, would need a sense of musicality. I initially tried a few designs including somewhat literal illustrations of music (sound waves, vinyl records, boom-boxes), but it quickly became clear that this wasn't enough to get at the heart of the book. The stories in *A Broken People's Playlist* aren't just about music. They're about people and their relationships—relationships with music and relationships with one another.

With this in mind, I commissioned illustrator Amrita Marino to create an original piece of art for the cover. Her expressive and explosively colorful work felt like the perfect fit. Amrita illustrated a cast of characters listening to music, DJing, singing, and dancing their way around the book jacket. I then added the finishing touch with some slightly off-kilter typography: the title ever moving and growing, like music getting louder, beckoning you out onto the dance floor.

Alicia Tatone

Here ends Chimeka Garricks's
A Broken People's Playlist.

The first edition of the book was printed and
bound at Lakeside Book Company
in Harrisonburg, Virginia, February 2023.

A NOTE ON THE TYPE

The text of this collection was set in Minion Pro, an OpenType update of the original 1990 Minion serif typeface, released in 2000. The original Minion serif typeface was designed by Robert Slimbach and released by Adobe Systems. Inspired by late Renaissance-era type, Minion's name stems from the traditional naming system for type sizes, in which minion is between nonpareil and brevier. Designed for body text, Minion is classic yet condensed in style, achieving a harmonious balance between the size of letters. It is a standard font in many Adobe programs, making it one of the most popular typefaces used in books.

HARPERVIA

An imprint dedicated to publishing international voices,
offering readers a chance to encounter other lives and other
points of view via the language of the imagination.